IN HOT WATER

At this time of morning, all the saloon girls were probably asleep after a long night of hustling drinks and servicing drunken cowboys and miners and freighters and townsmen. If he could slip into one of the rooms without waking whoever was inside, he might be able to wait out the manhunt.

Longarm opened the first door he came to and stepped inside with a silent, catlike grace that was unusual in such a big man. Unfortunately, his impressive stealth didn't do him a bit of good, because the girl inside this room was wide awake.

She was also naked as the day she was born and had just stepped out of a big tin tub full of hot, soapy water. That didn't stop her from picking up a gun from a chair next to the tub, pointing it at Longarm, and saying, "Take another step, cowboy, and I'll blow your damn head off."

FYE   11-29-06
RIVERDALE   UT

—————— ◆ TABOR EVANS ◆ ——————

LONGARM

AND THE RESTLESS REDHEAD

J

JOVE BOOKS, NEW YORK

THE BERKLEY PUBLISHING GROUP
Published by the Penguin Group
Penguin Group (USA) Inc.
375 Hudson Street, New York, New York 10014, USA
Penguin Group (Canada), 90 Eglinton Avenue East, Suite 700, Toronto, Ontario M4P 2Y3, Canada
(a division of Pearson Penguin Canada Inc.)
Penguin Books Ltd., 80 Strand, London WC2R 0RL, England
Penguin Group Ireland, 25 St. Stephen's Green, Dublin 2, Ireland (a division of Penguin Books Ltd.)
Penguin Group (Australia), 250 Camberwell Road, Camberwell, Victoria 3124, Australia
(a division of Pearson Australia Group Pty. Ltd.)
Penguin Books India Pvt. Ltd., 11 Community Centre, Panchsheel Park, New Delhi—110 017, India
Penguin Group (NZ), Cnr. Airborne and Rosedale Roads, Albany, Auckland 1310, New Zealand
(a division of Pearson New Zealand Ltd.)
Penguin Books (South Africa) (Pty.) Ltd., 24 Sturdee Avenue, Rosebank, Johannesburg 2196,
South Africa

Penguin Books Ltd., Registered Offices: 80 Strand, London WC2R 0RL, England

This is a work of fiction. Names, characters, places, and incidents either are the product of the author's imagination or are used fictitiously, and any resemblance to actual persons, living or dead, business establishments, events, or locales is entirely coincidental.

LONGARM AND THE RESTLESS REDHEAD

A Jove Book / published by arrangement with the author

PRINTING HISTORY
Jove edition / April 2006

Copyright © 2006 by The Berkley Publishing Group

ISBN: 0-515-14122-4

JOVE®
Jove Books are published by The Berkley Publishing Group,
a division of Penguin Group (USA) Inc.,
375 Hudson Street, New York, New York 10014.
JOVE is a registered trademark of Penguin Group (USA) Inc.
The "J" design is a trademark belonging to Penguin Group (USA) Inc.

PRINTED IN THE UNITED STATES OF AMERICA

10 9 8 7 6 5 4 3 2 1

Chapter 1

Longarm groaned as he rolled over and wondered where he was. This wasn't the first time in his eventful life that he had awoken from a sound sleep and not known exactly where he as. It hadn't happened in quite a while, though. Most of the time he held his liquor well enough so his brain didn't get muddled.

But not on this occasion. His head pounded fiercely, like there was a herd of crazed monkeys beating on the inside of his skull with ball-peen hammers.

He had a bad taste in his mouth, too. It couldn't have been much worse if a skunk had crawled in there and died. He opened and closed his mouth, trying to work up some spit so he could hang his head off the bed and expectorate into the chamber pot. That might not get rid of the taste, but he had to try it. The problem was, his mouth was as dry as a bale of cotton. His tongue felt like it was swollen up as big as a cotton bale, too.

He let out another groan as he sat up and swung his legs out of bed. Light struck his eyes and made him wince. Sunlight slanted in through a frowsy curtain that moved gently in the breeze coming through the room's single window. Longarm looked down at his feet. They rested on a thread-

1

bare rug. He was in a hotel room and not a very fancy one, at that.

He was also naked, and as he shifted a little on the lumpy mattress, raising his hands to press the balls of them against his throbbing temples, something rolled against his bare back. He turned his head and saw long, slim, smoothly naked legs stretched out on the mattress.

Even as bad as he felt, a smile touched his mouth under the sweeping longhorn mustache. He didn't recall climbing into bed with a gal the night before, but obviously he had. The polite thing would be to turn around and say howdy-do.

What he saw when he did so made him leap up from the bed and take a hurried step backward, his eyes widening in surprise. The thin rug under his feet slipped and threw him off-balance. Before he could catch himself, he sat down hard, bruising his bare rump on the unforgiving planks of the floor.

That put his head at just the right level so that he was staring into the sightless eyes of the dead woman in the bed.

She was young and lushly shaped and had a thick mass of auburn curls. She would have been damned attractive if it hadn't been for the fact that her throat was cut from ear to ear.

Longarm's face was grim as he climbed back to his feet and kicked the rug aside so that he wouldn't trip over it again. There was no need to check the woman for a pulse. The wound in her throat and the amount of blood that had leaked out of it and soaked the bed made it clear that she was a goner.

As he stared at her, Longarm absentmindedly reached up and tugged his right earlobe, then ran his thumbnail along the line of his rugged jaw. He thought hard, trying to remember who she was and figure out how in the hell he had wound up in bed with her corpse. No answers came to him.

Suddenly realizing that he was standing there naked as a jaybird, he looked around for his clothes. He found them

2

lying on a ladder-back chair in front of a scarred dressing table with a fly-specked mirror attached to it. When he looked in the mirror he saw a reflection of the dead woman in the bed, and it wasn't any prettier a picture that way.

Forcing himself not to look at her for a moment, he pulled on the bottom half of a pair of long underwear and some denim trousers. A butternut shirt lay on the chair as well, and a denim jacket was draped over the back, along with a gunbelt and holstered Colt. A flat-crowned, snuff-brown Stetson sat on the dressing table, and a pair of high-topped black boots stood beside the chair. It was the sort of get-up a drifting cowboy might wear . . .

But he wasn't a cowboy. Was he?

For a disconcerting second or two, Longarm wasn't sure. His mind was even more muddled than he had imagined.

But his thoughts cleared rapidly, and even though there were gaps in his memory, he knew good and well who he was: Deputy United States Marshal Custis Long, assigned to the Denver office of Chief Marshal Billy Vail.

He wasn't in Denver now. He didn't know exactly where he was, but he was sure of that much, anyway.

Taking a deep breath, Longarm picked up his shirt and shrugged into it, buttoning it quickly and tucking it in his trousers. He knew he would feel better if he was dressed, and the delay wasn't going to hurt the woman in the bed. She couldn't get any more dead.

The gunbelt seemed the next most important thing. Longarm strapped it on. The Colt rode easily on his left hip, butt forward, in a cross-draw rig. Longarm took the gun out of the holster for a moment, somehow reassured by the familiar feeling of the smooth walnut grips against his hand. Then he pouched the six-shooter and sat down to pull on his socks and boots.

When that was done, he stood and picked up his jacket. So far he hadn't come across the little leather folder that contained his badge and identification papers. Without those bona fides, he couldn't prove that he was a lawman.

But the jacket's inside pocket was empty. So were the outside ones, and the pockets in Longarm's shirt and trousers as well. Feeling his pulse start to pound a little harder, he stepped over to the dresser and picked up his hat.

Nothing stashed in there, either.

Where the hell was his badge?

The sight of the redheaded corpse had sort of shocked him sober, but he still felt rotten. The feeling grew stronger as he realized that he didn't have any identification of any sort. He could explain to the local star-packers who he really was, of course, but would they believe him?

It never entered his mind that he might have been responsible for the woman's death. He upheld the law; he didn't break it. Well, not too much, anyway, and then he usually just bent it a mite whenever it got in the way of him bringing some varmint to justice.

But if he wasn't able to prove his identity, the local law might blame him for this killing and try to throw him in the *juzgado*. Longarm couldn't allow that to happen. He had to find out who had killed the redhead and how she had wound up in bed with him. While he was at it, it would probably help if he figured out where he was and why he had come here.

Those were all damned good questions, but the sudden thudding of boots in the corridor outside warned Longarm that he wasn't going to have time to answer them right now. Something about the hurried sounds told him the footsteps were on their way here, to this room, where he was standing beside a bed containing a beautiful but very dead redhead, and him without any identification or excuses.

There was, however, the handle of a knife sticking out from under the bed. He noticed it when he glanced down. Stooping quickly, he peered under the bed and saw the sticky red coating on the blade. Yep, that was the weapon

4

that had done the job, all right. One more nail in his coffin.

Running away from trouble went against the grain for him. He was a lawman, after all, and had been one for a long time.

But this was as neat a frame-up as he had ever seen, and he knew that if he allowed himself to be arrested, he might never see the outside of a jail cell again . . . until the lynch mob came to drag him out and string him up. There *would* be a lynch mob. He was sure of that. Whoever had put him in this hole would see to it.

Those thoughts flashed through his brain in an instant, as the heavy footsteps came on down the hall toward the door of this room. Longarm snatched up his hat and jammed it on his head, then pulled on his jacket as he stepped over to the window.

The footsteps stopped outside the door as he swept the curtain aside and looked out. This room seemed to be at the back of the hotel—whatever hotel this was—and the window looked out on an alley and the blank rear wall of another building. The pane had been raised about six inches. Longarm put his hand under it and shoved it up the rest of the way as a fist began to bang on the door.

"Open up in there! There's been a report of trouble! Open the damn door!"

Longarm threw a leg over the sill. The room was on the second floor, with no fire stairs or anything else below the window except empty air.

Whoever was in the hall grabbed the knob and rattled it loudly, then shouted again, "Open up!"

The voice was vaguely familiar to Longarm, but he couldn't place it. The knowledge of who it belonged to was just one more thing that had fallen through the cracks of his memory. He climbed the rest of the way out of the window and hung from the sill by his hands.

He was tall enough so that the drop to the ground in the

alley wouldn't be too bad. He let go as a shoulder slammed against the door. Whoever was in the hall was trying to break it down now.

Longarm bent his knees as he landed, going down in a crouch to rob the fall of some of its momentum. The impact was still enough to rattle his teeth and jar his bones a little. His hat came off and landed in the dust. As he bent to pick it up, a gun cracked somewhere nearby and an ominous hum told him that a bullet had just passed close above his head.

Since he was already bent over, he kept going forward into a roll that took him behind a water barrel sitting against the wall of the building across the alley from the hotel. He snatched up his hat as he dove for cover, and as he fetched up behind the water barrel his Colt fairly leaped into his right hand. A second shot blasted and a slug thudded into the barrel.

Up on the second floor of the hotel, the door of the room containing the redhead's corpse smashed open. Longarm heard the sound through the open window. He didn't have time to glance in that direction, though, because he had the bushwhacker to deal with. He had already spotted the man crouched at the corner of the building, firing around it at him.

Catching a glimpse of shoulder, Longarm snapped a shot over the top of the water barrel and was rewarded by a splash of blood and a yelp of pain. The gunman staggered into view, his left arm dangling uselessly from a bullet-smashed shoulder. Yelling curses he charged at the barrel where Longarm knelt, triggering the gun in his other hand as he rushed forward.

The flurry of bullets smacked into the water barrel. A couple of them punched through it, and water began to spurt through the holes. Longarm rolled out from behind the barrel and wound up on his belly in the middle of the alley. He tipped up the barrel of his Colt and fired twice.

The slugs tore into the bushwhacker's chest and drove

him backward off his feet. Longarm would have preferred to take him alive and question him, but that wasn't an option at the moment. The motive for this ambush would have to remain a mystery for now.

Longarm had gotten a pretty good look at the gunman's hate-crazed face before the bullets knocked him sprawling, and the big deputy marshal knew he had never seen the man before—at least not that he remembered. The man looked like a typical hard case, with a blunt, beard-stubbled face and worn range clothes.

"Hey! Drop that gun!"

The shouted command came from the second-floor window in the hotel. Longarm looked up and saw a man standing there, the sun glinting on the star pinned to his vest. There was no way in hell Longarm was going to gun down a fellow lawman who was just doing his job.

So he threw a shot up there that chewed splinters from the side of the window and made the local badge-toter cuss and jump for cover. Longarm took advantage of the opportunity to surge to his feet and race down the alley, away from the window and the body of the bushwhacker, who hadn't moved since he went down.

Alert for more trouble, Longarm ducked around a corner and found himself in a narrow space between buildings. No one was in it at the moment, so he hurried along it toward a door in the side wall of the building to his right.

All those shots were bound to draw quite a bit of attention and soon. When he reached the door he tried the knob. It turned easily, so he opened the door and stepped through.

A little light came through a grimy window, enough to show him a stack of several empty whiskey crates and a couple of dusty tables, each with a cracked leg. This was some sort of storeroom in a saloon.

There was a door on the other side of the room. He crossed to it, listened for a second and didn't hear anything. His hand closed around the knob and turned it. He stepped out into a deserted hallway.

A narrow flight of stairs led up at the end of the hall to his right. Faintly, he heard shouting from outside somewhere as he walked toward the stairs. They were uncarpeted, just bare plank risers and steps. He went up them quickly, knowing that he needed to find a place where he could lie low until all the commotion died down. Then he could set about trying to find out what was going on here, so that he could clear his name.

At the top of the stairs, he found himself in another rear hallway. It was wider than the one below, and in the wall to his left were more grimy windows looking out over the alley where the shooting had taken place. To the right were several doors. If this really was a saloon, as he suspected, the doors probably led into rooms where the soiled doves who worked here took their customers.

At this time of the morning, all the saloon girls were probably asleep after a long night of hustling drinks and servicing drunken cowboys and miners and freighters and townsmen. If he could slip into one of the rooms without waking whoever was inside, he might be able to wait out the manhunt. The possibility wasn't all that far-fetched; a lot of saloon girls used opium, and nothing short of Gabriel's trumpet was going to wake them easily.

Longarm opened the first door he came to and stepped inside with a silent, catlike grace that was unusual in such a big man. Unfortunately, his impressive stealth didn't do him a bit of good, because the girl inside this room was wide awake.

She was also naked as the day she was born and had just stepped out of a big tin tub full of hot, soapy water. That didn't stop her from picking up a gun from a chair next to the tub, pointing it at Longarm, and saying, "Take another step, cowboy, and I'll blow your damn head off."

Chapter 2

Even with a gun pointed at him, Longarm couldn't help but notice how pretty the girl was. And how naked. Water ran off of her body and dripped onto the rug at her feet, and in a few places little dabs of soapsuds still clung to her smooth, wet skin.

She was a little bit of a thing, below medium height and slender, but the curve of her hips and the firm, apple-shaped breasts that rode proudly on her chest were plenty of evidence that she was full-grown. She had pinned up her raven-black hair before getting into the tin tub, but a few stands of it had come loose and hung freely around her heart-shaped face. The dark hair and the slight olive tint to her skin told Longarm that she had some Latin blood in her, but she also owned a pair of the most startlingly blue eyes he had ever seen.

The gun she held so steadily in her small first was no dainty lady's pocket pistol. It was a Colt Navy, single-action, .36 caliber, and thoroughly capable of putting a lethal hole in a man. She looked like she knew how to use it, too.

"No need to get all het up, ma'am," Longarm said.

"I'll be the judge of that," she snapped. "Some unwashed cowboy comes sauntering into a lady's boudoir just as she's finishing her morning bath. That sounds to me like he's looking for trouble."

"Farthest thing from my mind," Longarm assured her. "I'm a peaceable man. Matter of fact, I'm trying to avoid trouble."

"Is that so? That sounds like the law must be after you."

Dang, she was a sharp one. She had put that theory together in a hurry. And she was right about it, too, of course.

"I didn't do anything wrong—"

"Other than intrude here, where you're not wanted."

"I'd be glad to turn around and leave," Longarm offered. Maybe he could find sanctuary in one of the other rooms.

"I don't think so," she said coldly. "I think I'll just hold you here and see what Sheriff Thacker has to say about you."

Longarm's jaw tightened. He couldn't allow her to turn him in to the local authorities. This Sheriff Thacker might be a good lawman, but Longarm doubted if he would believe what had really happened . . . especially since he was probably the one who had busted down the door of that hotel room. He would have seen the redhead's body, and he would be the one who jumped back from the window when it appeared that Longarm was trying to plug him.

"Now," the girl went on, "if you've had your fill of looking . . ."

To tell the truth, under other circumstances Longarm wouldn't have minded gazing at her a while longer. She looked mighty fine with her clothes off. He was afraid, though, that he was going to have to jump her, knock that gun aside before she could ventilate him and try to corral her before she could raise a ruckus. It was going to be quite a challenge.

His muscles had just begun to tense so that he could leap toward her when she suddenly laughed and lowered

10

the gun. She said, "Oh, my, Custis, you looked so startled. I didn't think I could keep from laughing. You didn't really think I was going to shoot you, did you? I thought you were just playing along with me."

She set the gun on the chair and stepped toward him. This room had no windows, but there was a lamp on a night table beside the bed, and the light from it glowed warmly on her still-damp skin.

"Well, I was, uh, a mite thrown off stride," Longarm admitted.

She raised her hands to her head to unpin her hair. That caused her breasts to lift enticingly. The small, dark brown nipples were erect.

A shake of her head caused thick waves of black hair to tumble around her face. She was even more beautiful that way. As she moved closer to Longarm, he smelled the clean, fresh scent that clung to her skin. She reached up and rested her hands on his cheeks. The warmth of her touch made her irresistible as she pulled his face down to hers.

"Have you recovered enough to kiss me, cowboy?" she whispered.

"I reckon I have." He still had no idea who she was, but clearly she knew him, and pretty doggone well at that, considering how she was acting now.

Mystery or not, he figured that when a beautiful, young, nude gal wanted you to kiss her, a good rule of thumb was that you ought to go ahead and oblige her and figure out the rest of it later. He put a hand behind her head, burying it in that lustrous dark hair, and brought his mouth down on hers.

She responded eagerly, pressing her warm, sweet lips to his with an urgency that communicated itself to him. Instinctively, his arms went around her and drew her closer to him. She was tiny, almost dolllike in his embrace, but there was nothing fragile about her. She clung to him with a fierce strength that wouldn't be denied and kissed him with all the enthusiasm of a hot-blooded woman who knew what she wanted.

Even at a moment such as this, a part of Longarm's brain was still alert. He listened for any sounds of alarm coming from behind either of the room's two doors. The second floor of the saloon was quiet, though.

He wondered if she had heard the shots in the back alley. She certainly wasn't acting spooked.

When she finally broke the kiss, she gave him a coy smile and said, "I know what you want."

Figuring out where he was, what he was doing here and how he had come to be in bed with a murdered redhead would be a good start on what he wanted. Explaining all that didn't seem to be what she had in mind, though. She plucked a pillow off the bed and dropped it in front of him, then got down on her knees. Her fingers went to the buttons of his trousers and began deftly unfastening them.

Now, this was a dilemma. A few minutes earlier, he had been escaping from a murder frame-up and swapping lead with some hard case who wanted to kill him. That didn't leave a man in much of a mood for romping with a gal, no matter how pretty and how undressed she was.

On the other hand, he had come in here hoping to lie low for a while, and he didn't seem to be attracting any undue attention from anybody except this brazen young woman who obviously meant him no harm. What she meant was to give him a French lesson, and for the life of him, he couldn't see what it would hurt.

He was already rock-hard. The kissing and fondling of her he had done had been enough to see to that. She freed his erection from his trousers and let the shaft spring out proudly from his groin. Wrapping her hands around it—or trying to, anyway—she laughed softly and said, "My God,

Custis, have you grown? I think it's even bigger than it was the other times."

So this *wasn't* the first time for them. That was good to know. Every little bit of information helped. A fella never knew what would be the key that unlocked his fuzzy memory.

The girl leaned forward, and her pink, delicate tongue lightly circled the crown of his long, thick pole. Then she planted teasing kisses all around it and along the shaft. Longarm's jaw was tight with desire. He rested his hands on her shoulders as she continued her light, tantalizing touches.

She was mighty good at what she was doing. Longarm felt his arousal building quickly. She worked him up to a fever pitch and then leaned back to let him subside a little before she embarked on another round of caresses with her lips and tongue. Longarm growled deep in his throat, unsure how much more of this he could withstand.

Finally she opened her mouth wide and took him in. As petite as she was, he wasn't sure just how much she could manage, but she did just fine. Better than fine, actually. His fingers tangled in her hair as her head began to bob up and down in front of his groin.

After only a few moments, his climax thundered out of him, blasting from his shaft as the girl jerked her head back and gasped in a passionate surge of her own. Most of Longarm's juices landed on her breasts, but there was also a white strand on her chin. She reached around him and grabbed on tight to his buttocks as a shudder of culmination ran through her.

Longarm's pulse hammered in his head. He was a mite shaken himself. That had been quite a climax, and it left him a little weak in the knees. He took a deep breath.

The girl held her hands up to him. He took them and pulled her to her feet. She wiped her chin, gave him a smile that managed to be somehow sweetly innocent and utterly wanton at the same time, and said, "I hope the water's still a little warm. I'm going to have to wash off again after that." She paused. "Would you like to join me, Custis?"

It was a tempting invitation, but stripping off his clothes—and gunbelt—and climbing into that tub with her would leave him more vulnerable than he wanted to be right now. He still didn't know if his pursuers would catch up to him.

"You go ahead," he told her. "I might sit and watch, though."

"Well, I should hope so." She tucked his now-soft organ back inside his trousers, buttoned them up, and gave him a little pat. Then she walked over to the tub with an extra-saucy sway of her hips and stepped into the water again.

Longarm picked up a chair from in front of a dressing table, reversed it, and straddled it. He watched as the girl sank into the water, fished out a sponge, and started washing herself. It was a sight to see. The water covered part of her breasts, but her nipples kept flirting with the surface.

"I wasn't sure I'd see you again so soon," she said. "After all, it was only last night that we . . ."

She left the sentence unfinished and gave him that smile again.

So he had been with her the night before. Obviously, it had been after that when he went to bed in the hotel. And after *that* when the dead woman had been placed in bed with him. He didn't know everything, but he sure as hell knew that he wouldn't have climbed between the sheets with a corpse if he had known about it.

There was only one conclusion he could draw from that: somebody had slipped him a Mickey Finn, named after the Barbary Coast saloon-keeper who made a sideline out of shanghaiing unsuspecting sailors. The headache and the bad taste in his mouth when he woke up had already made Longarm suspect that he'd been drugged. Now that

14

he had time to think through the sequence of events, it was inescapable.

He frowned as another thought occurred to him. If he had been with this dark-haired girl *before* he'd been drugged, wasn't it entirely possible that she had been the one who had given him the knockout drops?

"Custis, what's wrong?" she asked from the tub. "You look positively solemn."

He didn't want to give anything away, so he forced a grin onto his face and waved a hand casually. "Aw, it was nothing," he said. "I was just thinking that a gal doesn't have a right to be as downright pretty as you are right now."

"You flatterer." She sat up a little straighter, bringing her breasts completely out of the water. "Oh! I'm getting my hair wet. I forgot that I had taken it down."

She ran the sponge over her breasts and then dropped it in the water again. When she stood up, the water drained off as it had before, leaving droplets sparkling in the dark triangle of fine-spun hair between her thighs.

"Why don't you get that towel and come over here and dry me?" she suggested, pointing to a folded white towel that sat on the dressing table.

That sounded reasonable enough to Longarm. He stood up from the chair and stepped over to the dressing table. As he picked up the towel, he realized that it had been sitting on top of a newspaper. Words printed on the masthead proclaimed it to be the *Weekly Medallion,* published every Saturday in Medallion, Arizona. Claude Brandstett, editor and publisher.

Longarm's breath hissed between his teeth. Medallion, Arizona, sounded awfully familiar. Was that where he was? There was no guarantee of that just because the girl had a newspaper from there in her room. Maybe Medallion was her hometown, and she had brought the paper from there. Maybe one of her customers had left it behind . . . although, to tell the truth, Longarm wasn't sure she was a typical saloon girl who brought gents up here and bedded them for money. Something about her seemed different, despite the surroundings.

But he had definitely heard of Medallion before. He was sure of that. And when he thought of the name, he thought of something else.

Trouble.

Why would he associate trouble with Medallion, Arizona, unless it was his job that had brought him there? He was a deputy U.S. marshal, he reminded himself. Trouble was his business.

"Custis?" the girl said from the tub. "What's wrong? I thought you were going to dry me."

Longarm tore his gaze away from the newspaper, even though he wanted to pick it up and study everything that was written on its front page in the hope that it would restore even more of his memory. He didn't want the girl to get suspicious of him, though. He would continue to play along with her and try to get his hands on the paper later. . . .

He turned around with the towel in his hands and went toward her as she stepped out of the tub, so that made it difficult for him to reach for his gun when the door was kicked open and yet another hombre Longarm had never seen before charged in, mad as hell.

Chapter 3

The man was a big, strapping cowboy with a shock of
blond hair under a cuffed-back Stetson, and as he looked
back and forth between Longarm and the girl, his face, already flushed, grew even darker with anger.

"I knew it!" he roared. "I knew I heard a man's voice in
here! Damn it, Connie, don't I mean anything to you?"

"Get out of here, Brice," the girl said, her voice cool.
"This is none of your business."

"The hell it ain't!" The cowboy's hands clenched into
big fists as he turned toward Longarm. "I'm gonna bust this
bastard wide open!"

Longarm doubted that. He and Brice were pretty much
the same size, and while the cowboy was brawnier, there
was plenty of strength built into Longarm's rangy, raw-
boned frame. Brice lunged at him, launching a roundhouse
blow as he came.

Longarm flipped the big white towel over Brice's head,
blinding him and turning his bulllike charge into an awkward stumble. Stepping to the side, Longarm stuck out a
leg and swept Brice's feet out from under him. The cowboy
went down, crashing to the floor with stunning force.

The fall didn't keep him down for long. He surged up, ripping the towel off his head as he came to his feet.

He stopped short, though, as he found himself looking into the barrel of Longarm's Colt.

The big lawman was flat out of patience. Too much was happening too quickly, and the drug-induced gaps in his memory made it impossible for him to keep up with what was going on. Everything needed to just settle down so that he could get his wits back about him.

"Take it easy, old son," he told Brice in a hard voice. "I'd hate like hell to have to shoot you."

Brice swallowed hard as he stared down the muzzle of the six-gun. He worked up a sneer and said, "You wouldn't dare. If you pull that trigger, the crew of the Triangle C will have you strung up before the sun goes down. That is, if the boys don't rope you between some horses and tear you limb from limb."

"That'd be a gruesome fate, all right," agreed Longarm, "but whatever happens to me, it won't matter to you, since you'd be dead already."

"Yeah, there is that," Brice said grudgingly. "Ease up on that trigger, all right?"

Connie had climbed back in the tub and sunk down into the water. "Excuse me," she said. "If you're not going to kill each other, could one of you hand me that towel?"

Longarm gestured with the barrel of the Colt. Brice sighed and reached down to pick up the towel from where he had slung it on the floor. He turned to hand it to Connie as she stood up. Longarm saw the way his eyes played over her wet, naked body. The longing in them was almost painful.

Connie took the towel and wrapped it around herself as she stepped out of the tub for the third time. She was small enough so that the towel completely enveloped her.

"I told you, Brice, you don't have any claim on me," she

said to the cowboy. "Just because we had a little fun doesn't mean I'm ready to marry you or anything."

"I could give you a good life, Connie," he said miserably. "I've been takin' some of my pay from Walt in livestock, and he's gonna let me use some of his range to graze it. There's a line shack there I could fix up real nice, and in a year or two I'll have enough money saved up to buy the land outright. It'd be our spread, free and clear."

"You know I'm not interested in being a ranch wife." Connie shook her head. "You just can't get that through your head, can you?"

Longarm had heard enough to know that these two were involved in some sort of domestic drama of their own. He broke in to the conversation, saying, "You reckon I can put this gun away now without having to worry about needing to shoot you, mister?"

Brice gave him a distracted nod. "Yeah, yeah." His eyes narrowed as he looked at Connie. "I guess I shouldn't blame you just because my gal's a . . . a strumpet!"

Her eyes blazed with anger as she stepped closer to him and her hand flashed up in a stinging slap across his face. She might be small, but she packed a surprising wallop. Brice jerked back, his cheek turning a bright red where she had struck him.

"I won't stand for that kind of talk," she said. "Get out."

"Damn it, Connie—"

"You heard me."

Brice stared at her helplessly for a moment, then glanced at Longarm. He didn't get any encouragement from the big lawman, who hadn't holstered his Colt even though he had lowered it to his side. With a frustrated sigh, Brice said, "All right, but you're makin' a mistake, Connie." As he turned toward the door, he added to Longarm, "This ain't finished."

"That's where you're wrong," Longarm said.

Brice just glared at him and went on out of the room, slamming the door behind him.

As Longarm slipped his gun back in its holster, Connie said, "I'm sorry, Custis. I didn't know Brice was in town. I might have been a bit more . . . discreet if I had known."

"He's your regular gentleman friend, is he?"

"Well, he thinks he is, anyway." Connie shook her head. "It's complicated. Ever since I came here to Medallion, Brice has been mooning over me. He was in the audience the first time I sang downstairs. I saw him get calf-eyed then, and he's been courting me ever since."

"He seems to think it's serious."

Connie had the good grace to blush a little. "I let him take me for a buggy ride a few times. There's something about being out alone beside a stream, with a nice blanket and some thick grass and the scent of wildflowers in the air." She paused. "A girl gets carried away sometimes . . ."

Longarm held up a hand. "Say no more. No need to explain to me. I know all about folks getting carried away. Seems we were guilty of that ourselves just a few minutes ago."

"Yes, you could say that," Connie agreed with a laugh.

An awkward silence sprang up between them. Longarm thought about what she had just said—not the part about pitching woo on a creek bank, but about her coming here to Medallion and singing downstairs. That was confirmation that he *was* in Medallion, Arizona. Also, she was a singer, not a typical soiled dove. It was nice to know that his hunch about her had been correct, not that it had anything to do with his current situation.

"Well, I suppose I ought to get dressed," she finally said. "I can't just stand around in a towel all day."

"You look mighty fetching in it," Longarm told her.

"Maybe so, but I have things to do and I'm sure you do, too."

Yeah, like lying low and staying out of sight of the law. But he couldn't tell her that.

"I'm sure Mr. Jessup has all sorts of chores for you," Connie went on. "I know he and his wife came into town from the mine yesterday afternoon, otherwise you wouldn't have been around last night."

Jessup? Who in blazes was that? Somebody who had a mine, judging by what the girl had just said. Again, Longarm felt like he ought to remember these things, but the details were frustratingly elusive.

Clearly, though, according to Connie, Longarm worked for the mysterious Jessup, and since Longarm knew good and well he was a deputy marshal, that meant he was working undercover on a case. That was common practice with him. Billy Vail tossed a job in his lap, and he rode in to wherever without announcing who he really was, so that he could size up the situation before anybody knew that a federal lawman was around.

Give him enough time and he would put all the pieces of this puzzle together.

He might not have the time, though, if he was arrested for a murder he hadn't committed. He said, "I'm sort of tired, and I don't reckon Mr. Jessup will need me right away. If you don't mind, I might just stay here for a while."

He hoped he and Connie were friendly enough for such a request to seem reasonable.

"Oh, all right," she said. "The least you can do is set up the screen for me, though, so I can have a little privacy while I'm getting dressed." She pointed to a folding screen with an Oriental-looking design painted on it that stood in a corner of the room.

"Be glad to." Longarm picked up the screen and unfolded it, setting it up so that it blocked his view of the bed and the bathtub. There was a wardrobe on the other side of the bed which he couldn't see anymore, either.

Connie disappeared behind the screen as Longarm sat down again in the chair where he had been earlier. Women were funny critters. Connie hadn't seemed to mind at all standing stark naked in front of him and she sure hadn't been shy about that French lesson she'd given him, but she didn't want him watching while she put her clothes on.

That was all right, though, because she couldn't see him, either. He picked up that copy of the *Weekly Medallion* and began scanning the stories on the front page.

The first thing that caught his eyes was a write-up about a brawl in the Cattle King Saloon between cowboys from the Triangle C spread and miners from the Oro Grande Mine. That told Longarm that Medallion was a settlement caught between cattle and mining interests. The situation had cropped up in other places in the West, and it was nearly always a recipe for trouble.

Reading farther down in the story by Claude Brandstett, editor and publisher, Longarm found a quote from a fella named Victor Jessup, the owner of the Oro Grande. Jessup promised that his employees who had taken part in the fracas would be disciplined. But then he added a sly dig about his men being provoked by elements opposed to progress, namely the cowboys who worked for Walt Conroy.

It was unlikely there would be more than one big skookum he-wolf around Medallion named Jessup, so Longarm figured the mine owner was the man he supposedly worked for. He recalled Brice's mention of the Triangle C and somebody named Walt, who had to be the Walt Conroy who was mentioned in the newspaper story. Longarm wondered if Brice was one of the Triangle C cowboys who had busted up the Cattle King Saloon.

For that matter, he wondered if he was actually *in* the Cattle King Saloon at the moment. He would have asked Connie, but that would be a mighty suspicious question. He ought to know where he was.

"What are you doing, Custis?" she asked from behind the screen. "You haven't gone to sleep, have you?"

Longarm glanced up from the newspaper. He had been vaguely aware that she was humming quietly to herself, and he had heard her opening and closing the doors of the wardrobe and making other little sounds as she got dressed. The lamp was on the other side of the screen with Connie, and the screen was thin enough so that he could see her silhouette through it.

An intriguing silhouette it was, too, slender but curved in all the right places. Longarm said, "Nope, I'm awake. Just looking at the paper."

"That worthless rag! Did you see what Brandstett wrote about me?"

Longarm looked farther down the front page but didn't see any mention of Connie in any of the stories. "Nope."

"It's inside, on what passes for a society page. He said my new program of selections from *H.M.S. Pinafore* and *The Pirates of Penzance,* by Mr. Gilbert and Mr. Sullivan, was decidedly lacking. Hmmmph! The rest of the audience didn't seem to think so. I got *three* standing ovations, and that's a record for the Cattle King. Of course, I realize this is hardly an opera house, like the one they have in Denver, but still, it's the closest thing to it anybody is likely to find in Medallion."

Longarm grunted noncommittally, while mentally filing away the knowledge that this was indeed the Cattle King Saloon in which he found himself.

Another story on the front page mentioned Victor Jessup and the Oro Grande Mine again, and again it was bad news. A shipment of gold from the mine had been stolen by masked outlaws a few days earlier. Sheriff Rip Thacker was quoted as saying that although a posse had given chase to the thieves, they had been unable to track them down. Sheriff Thacker had no further leads to the bandits at this time, but he promised the investigation would continue. This was the sixth such gold shipment hijacking in the past three months, the story added.

Longarm frowned. Most of the gold that was mined went to the U.S. Mint, so when it was stolen that usually made it a matter for the Justice Department. Quite a few times in his career, he had been sent to find out who was to blame for stolen gold shipments and put a stop to it. It was entirely logical that Billy Vail had sent him to Medallion to investigate the robberies plaguing the Oro Grande. In that case it made sense that he might pretend to be working for the mine owner, Victor Jessup.

But did Jessup know he was a lawman, or had Longarm concealed that knowledge from him as well? It was damned difficult, not to mention frustrating, to have to put this all together on the fly, so to speak, while he was dodging a murder frame-up.

Connie came out from behind the screen wearing a neat, dark blue gown. She carried a hat of the same shade. She came over to the dressing table, pinned up her hair again, and settled the hat on top of it. She smiled down at Longarm and asked, "How do I look?"

"Positively elegant."

"Thank you." She held out a hand to him. "Now, come along."

"Where are we going?" Longarm asked.

"I'm going to give Claude Brandstett a piece of my mind. Imagine, calling any performance of mine lacking!"

Longarm had only one performance of hers to go by, but he certainly wouldn't have called it lacking. He said, "You better go on by yourself, darlin'. I'm liable to lose my temper and take a swing at the fella."

"Oh, you're so sweet, Custis!" She leaned over and gave him a peck on the forehead. "I'll be back later, and we can have some more fun."

"Sounds fine to me." Longarm was relieved that she

24

hadn't decided to argue and insist that he come with her. He wanted to stay up here for a while longer before he slipped out of the saloon and tried to figure out his next move.

Connie picked up a bag from the dressing table and went out the room's front door, smiling over her shoulder at Longarm as she left. He smiled back at her and waved, but as soon as the door was closed he returned to reading the newspaper.

The date on it was June 5. He didn't know what the date was, but the paper didn't seem very old. He thought it was almost freshly printed, in fact. That jibed with Connie's anger over Claude Brandstett's disparaging remarks.

He didn't glean anything else from the newspaper's front page, so he opened it up and started skimming through the interior columns. The only thing of interest he found in the local news was that several area ranches, the Triangle C among them, had reported losing cattle to rustlers. Lawlessness seemed to be rampant in these parts, mused Longarm. Rustling and gold robberies and saloon brawls . . . Sheriff Thacker wasn't doing a very good job of keeping the lid on.

Longarm turned to that society page Connie had mentioned. He saw the story that had gotten her so incensed and learned that she was billed as Miss Constance Maxwell. He would always think of her as Connie, he told himself wryly.

Looking farther down the page, the name Jessup leaped out at him again. The story mentioned a ball to be given at the home of Mr. and Mrs. Victor Jessup, and it referred to the "auburn-haired beauty" of Mrs. Jessup.

Longarm looked up from the paper with a frown, remembering the dead woman he had discovered in his bed a little more than an hour earlier. She had been a beauty when she was alive, and her hair was definitely auburn. But she couldn't possibly have been the wife of Victor Jessup, the owner of the Oro Grande Mine and Longarm's ostensible employer.

Could she?

Longarm had just started to wonder how he could go about getting a look at Mrs. Jessup when the knob of the room's rear door rattled slightly. Connie would have come in the front door, more than likely, and anyway, the stealth with which the knob slowly turned told Longarm that whoever was in the rear hall was trying to sneak into the room.

He set the paper aside and came lithely to his feet, reaching for his gun as he did so. His gaze darted around the room, searching for someplace to hide.

Chapter 4

A couple of long, catlike steps put Longarm behind the screen where Connie had gotten dressed earlier. Colt in hand, he bent and puffed out the flame in the lamp, so that he wouldn't be silhouetted through the thin screen the way she had been.

Then he waited, standing still and utterly silent. A few seconds later, the room's rear door swung open, and someone stepped inside. Longarm heard the faint creak of a floorboard.

The intruder didn't close the door. Instead he hissed, "Connie!" It was hard to tell much about the voice, only that it was male. The man said, "Connie, darling, are you here?"

Longarm's jaw tightened. The man couldn't see the bed from where he was. He would have to step around the screen in order to do that. Which meant that he would see Longarm standing there.

Longarm's hand tightened on the Colt. If he moved fast enough, he might be able to wallop the fella before the man got a good look at him. He hated to clout somebody he didn't even know, some poor bastard who had probably snuck up here for a tryst with the beautiful saloon singer, but he might not have any choice. He couldn't afford to be stuck behind bars right now.

The floorboards creaked again as the man came closer. Then footsteps sounded in the front corridor, and the man hurriedly withdrew, obviously afraid to take even the slightest chance of being caught here. The rear door clicked shut behind him.

Longarm turned his head to look at the front door. He had dodged being discovered by whoever had come in the back, but now he might be in danger from the other direction.

He relaxed as the footsteps went on past the door. They didn't have anything to do with Connie. But they had been enough to scare off the man who had come looking for her.

He pouched the iron and stepped out from behind the screen. Maybe waiting in here wasn't such a good idea after all. Connie's room seemed to be a busy place. He went to the rear door and put his ear against it, listening intently for a moment before he turned the knob and stepped out into that hall.

The corridor was deserted. Longarm headed for the rear stairs and went down them as quietly as he could. When he reached the first floor, instead of going to the storeroom where he had entered the building, he turned in the other direction. He didn't want to just retrace his steps and run smack-dab into the local law.

There were two doors at the end of the hall. Slowly and carefully, he turned the knob of the left-hand one and opened the door just a crack. Putting an eye to the gap, he looked out into the main room of the Cattle King Saloon.

Although it was difficult to be sure from such a narrow perspective, he thought it was a big, sprawling place, with long bars on both walls and lots of tables. A few men stood at the bar drinking and one desultory poker game was going on at a table, but it was too early in the day for the saloon to be doing much business.

Longarm eased the door shut. Even with only a few men

in the saloon, he couldn't just walk out through there as big as you please. Somebody was bound to remember him. They might even be looking for him already, if the sheriff had spread the word about the dead woman.

He tried the other door. It was unlocked, too, and when he opened it he could dimly see that it led to a short flight of four or five steps. At the top of the steps was a stage, also very dimly lit. Longarm figured the curtain was drawn, and a little light from the saloon's main room came through the gaps around it. That would be where Connie did her singing.

Longarm slipped through the door and closed it behind him. He didn't know what was on the other side of the stage, but he was going to find out. He needed a discreet way out of this place.

As quietly as he could, he went up the steps and across the stage, staying toward the rear of it, well away from the purple velvet curtain. He thought the curtain was thick enough so that it would muffle any slight sounds he might make. He could just barely hear the men in the saloon talking.

When he reached the wings on the far side of the stage, he looked for another exit and found one tucked into a dark corner. It was locked, but the key was in the lock and he turned it, hearing the tumblers click over. When he eased the door open slightly, he saw that it led into another alley. He was on the far side of the saloon from the hotel where he had woken up next to the dead redhead.

Longarm stepped into the alley and pulled the door closed behind him. Even though he knew he wasn't out of danger, he felt a sense of relief go through him. He preferred being out in the open, where he could move around, to skulking through the rear corridors of a saloon. Now he could try to blend in with the citizens of Medallion and figure out what to do next.

He walked toward the main street. When he got to the

mouth of the alley he paused and looked around. He saw buckboards parked front of the general mercantile and the hardware store. Across the street was an assay office. Down the block he saw the sign for the offices of the *Weekly Medallion*. From where he was, he couldn't see the sheriff's office and jail, but he figured they were around somewhere.

Quite a few people were moving around on the street. Cowboys on horseback ambled past, and men with the look of hard-rock miners strode along the boardwalks. There were a few women in evidence, too, apparently going about their daily marketing.

But nobody seemed to display any sense of urgency or act like anything out of the ordinary was going on. Longarm had expected to see the sheriff and his deputies conducting a manhunt, searching for the man who had cut the throat of the woman in the hotel room and then gunned down a man in the alley out back.

Of course, Longarm was only responsible for one of those killings, but the local star-packers wouldn't know that.

Instead, the settlement didn't appear to be up in arms at all. Longarm frowned. That didn't make sense. Even in rough-and-tumble frontier towns, women didn't get their throats cut every day. That should have caused some commotion, even though the gunning down of some drifting hard case might not.

What the hell was going on here?

Longarm knew he wouldn't find the answer to that question by lurking in an alley. He took a deep breath and moved out, stepping up onto the boardwalk. A glance past the Cattle King showed him the sign in front of the hotel, which was called the Horton House. Longarm turned the other direction. He kept his head down, the wide brim of his hat shielding his face.

He walked past a saddle maker's shop and a land office.

That brought him opposite the newspaper office. Just as he reached that point, the door of the office opened. Longarm turned toward the building on his side of the street, putting his back toward the newspaper office in case Connie emerged from it.

He could see the door reflected in the window where he stood. A man stepped out of it, not Connie, so Longarm relaxed a little. The man was stocky, with bushy muttonchop whiskers, and wore a suit and bowler hat. Longarm wondered if he was Claude Brandstett, the editor and publisher.

The man in the bowler hat hurried off after closing the door behind him. Longarm supposed Connie had already been to the newspaper office to lodge her complaint and was gone. She might be back in her room on the second floor of the Cattle King by now, or she might be off running some other errands. If she *had* gone back to the saloon, he wondered if she'd been surprised—and disappointed—to find him gone.

He strolled on, aware that no one seemed to be paying the least bit of attention to him. That gave him a chance to look around Medallion and familiarize himself with the town. The main street was half a dozen blocks long, with an equal number of cross streets. It ran east and west along a shoulder of flat land at the base of a mountain that loomed to the north. There were other mountains stretching off to the west, with snowcapped peaks and heavily timbered lower slopes. To the south of town, the land shelved off into flatter, drier terrain that still had enough graze on it to make it suitable for ranching.

A large, square, stone building stood at the west end of the main street. That would be the courthouse, sheriff's office, and jail, Longarm decided. Looking the other way, at the east end of the street, he saw that the road forked. The left-hand branch curved and led to a large house set up the slope a short distance so that it overlooked the town. It was a fancy place, with lots of turrets and dormer windows and a well-kept lawn surrounding it. A house like that had to belong to a rich man. Longarm recalled the newspaper story about the ball to be held at Victor Jessup's mansion. He had a hunch that mansion was what he was looking at now.

Connie had said something about Jessup and his wife coming into town from the mine. Longarm looked up at the mountain looming over the town. The Oro Grande was probably up there somewhere, and judging by what Connie had said, the Jessups had a house up there, too, probably smaller than the mansion here in Medallion.

The sound of a lot of hoofbeats drew Longarm's attention. He looked back down the street to the west and saw close to a dozen riders come around a corner and head in his direction. They stopped before they reached him, however, reining to a halt in front of the Cattle King. They were led by a tall, lean, middle-aged man with a gray mustache. He dismounted and looped his reins around the hitch rail in front of the saloon. The other men followed suit.

Somebody stepped through the batwings onto the boardwalk. Longarm recognized the cowboy called Brice. He wondered if the hombre had been downstairs drinking ever since Connie had thrown him out of her room. Brice lifted a hand in greeting and said something to the leader of the newcomers. Longarm suspected that man was Walt Conroy, the owner of the Triangle C.

One of the other riders stepped onto the boardwalk as well, cuffing back a tan hat so that it hung from its chin strap between its owner's shoulder blades. Longarm was surprised when a thick mass of blond hair tumbled down around the rider's shoulders. That wasn't a fella at all, but a lithe, slender woman. She wore range clothes like the others, and as she turned slightly, Longarm could see how the fabric of the faded red shirt hugged her breasts.

The whole bunch went inside the Cattle King. Longarm walked on down the street. Several doors past the newspaper office, he saw a neat frame building with a sign on it that read: ORO GRANDE MINING COMPANY — HEADQUARTERS.

So that was Jessup's office. Maybe Jessup was there. Longarm figured it was time he got a look at his "boss." He started across the street.

The rattle of wheels and the swift rataplan of hoof-beats made him pause. He turned to his right as a stage-coach came around a nearby corner and rolled straight toward him.

Longarm stepped back quickly to avoid being trampled by the leaders of the stagecoach team. Up on the driver's box, a bearded old jehu kicked the brake lever and hauled back on the reins as he shouted, "Whoa there, you con-sarned jugheads!"

The coach came to an abrupt stop, swaying a little on the broad leather thoroughbraces that ran underneath it. The cloud of dust that had billowed out behind it caught up and washed over the stage, making the driver cough.

"Dagnab it!" he said. "Like to choke a feller to death!" He dropped nimbly from the box and strode toward Long-arm. "Why don't you watch where you're goin', you long-legged jackrabbit? Why, for two bits I'd—"

He stopped short and gazed up at Longarm through rheumy eyes. He was short, and his bowed legs made him look even shorter. He wore a buckskin vest with silver con-chos on it over a red plaid flannel shirt. The sleeves of the shirt were rolled up to reveal the cuffs of long underwear. A holster containing an old Dragoon Colt was supported by a sagging gunbelt. The old-timer's boots had seen better days, too, as had the felt hat with the pushed-up brim that perched on his head. His face was brown and weathered, which made the bristling white beard on his jaws and chin stand out that much more.

"Dang it, Custis," he said, "I like to run you down!"

Longarm had recognized him immediately. With a

smile, the big lawman said, "Hello, Salty. I didn't expect to run into you here in Medallion."

A few years earlier, during a case Longarm had been assigned to in the southern part of Arizona Territory, he had made the acquaintance of this old-timer who more than lived up to his nickname, which was actually the only name Longarm knew him by. Salty had proven to be quite a help to him during that dust-up, and he was glad to see the old pelican again.

Salty squinted at him and said, "What do you mean by that? You knowed I was hereabouts. I'm the reg'lar driver on the run from Kingman to Medallion. Remember how you stepped in and stopped that stage holdup a couple o' days ago?"

Longarm didn't remember anything of the sort, although again it seemed that the incident Salty referred to *ought* to be familiar to him. He figured he could trust Salty—the old-timer already knew that he was a federal lawman—and he was about to explain that something had happened to cause some holes in his memory when an imperious voice called, "Parker! Stay right there, Parker!"

"Uh-oh," muttered Salty. "Here comes trouble."

Chapter 5

Longarm and Salty both turned to look toward the Oro
Grande Mining office. The man who strode toward them
from that direction wore a gray suit and a black Stetson. A
diamond stickpin glittered in his silk cravat. As he came up
he took a cigar from his vest pocket and put it in his mouth.
Strong teeth clamped down on the cylinder of tightly rolled
tobacco. He said around it, "I've been looking for you,
Parker."

Longarm knew that comment was directed at him. As
soon as the man had called out that name, the big lawman's
brain had gone into high gear. Often when he was working
undercover, he used the name Custis Parker, since
"Parker" actually was his middle name. This stranger's
garb, and the fact that he had come from the Oro Grande
office, told Longarm there was a strong likelihood he was
Victor Jessup. And Jessup's use of the name Parker meant
that Longarm probably hadn't informed the mine owner of
his true identity.

That was the way he was going to play it, anyway. He
said, "I've been around town."

"That's fine, but right now I need you to come up to the

35

house with me and see about arrangements for the party tonight."

Longarm nodded slowly and said, "All right."

The mention of a party was one more bit of evidence indicating that his hunch about the man's identity was correct. Victor Jessup and his wife were supposed to host some sort of soiree, according to the newspaper, and obviously it was scheduled for tonight. Longarm had no idea what sort of "arrangements" Jessup expected him to make, however. He had no experience planning fancy parties. The whole idea was worthy of a horselaugh.

The man took the cigar out of his mouth and said, "Hello, Salty."

The old-timer bobbed his head in a nod. "Mornin', Mr. Jessup."

"No more trouble from outlaws since the other day, I hope?"

"No, sir. I reckon Custis here scared off all the road agents in these parts."

Longarm wondered how in blazes he had done that.

"Yes, it was lucky Parker came along when he did." Jessup replaced the cigar in his mouth and jerked his head toward a buggy parked in front of the mining office. "Let's go."

Longarm felt an instinctive dislike for the man, although he had to admit that Jessup had an impressive vitality about him. The mine owner was around fifty, with a broad, ruddy face and salt-and-pepper hair. He looked like he was in good enough shape that he could have gone down in a mine shaft and swung a sledgehammer with his employees if he had to. He strode quickly over to the buggy, but Longarm didn't have any trouble keeping up with him.

Meanwhile Salty climbed back onto the driver's box of the coach and got the big Concord rolling down the street again toward the stage line office. Longarm was sorry to see him go. He had been hoping to pick the old pelican's brain in order to find out what was going on around here. It looked like that would have to wait, though. For the time being, Longarm would have to continue navigating the murky waters of this case by the seat of his pants.

They reached the buggy and Jessup motioned for Longarm to climb in. Longarm wondered if he was supposed to take the reins. Jessup solved that problem for him by grabbing the reins himself.

Before they could get moving, the man in the bowler hat Longarm had seen earlier hurried along the boardwalk toward them and lifted a hand to stop them.

"Mr. Jessup," the man called. "Could I talk to you for a minute?"

"What is it, Brandstett?" Jessup asked.

The newspaperman took a pad of paper and a stub of a pencil from an inside coat pocket. "Do you have any last-minute comments about the ball tonight?"

"You'd have to ask my wife about that," Jessup said curtly. "It's mostly her fandango, not mine."

"But you know the guest list, of course. I assume the other mine owners from the area will be in attendance?"

"That's right."

"What about Walt Conroy? As the owner of the largest ranch in this part of the territory, he's certainly an influential man."

Jessup snorted in contempt. "He doesn't hold any influence with me. They say that all money spends the same, but somehow I've never been able to stomach a greenback or a double eagle that has the stink of cow dung on it."

Brandstett smiled. "Can I quote you on that, Mr. Jessup?"

"You can quote me on any damned thing you please." Jessup lifted the reins. "Now you'll have to excuse me. I've got things to do."

He slapped the leathers against the backs of the two fine black horses hitched to the buggy and as the animals got moving he pulled them in a tight turn that headed the vehicle toward the big house just east of town. Longarm thought that Jessup handled the team well, but that didn't really change his opinion of the man. He said, "Sounds like you and this fella Conroy don't get along too well."

"Of course not," Jessup grated around the cigar. He glanced over at Longarm. "You ought to know that. His stinking cowhands pick fights any time my men come into town, and I'm still not convinced that it wasn't some of his men who tried to hold up the stage the other day. The way they were masked, nobody could recognize them."

Longarm nodded as if he knew what Jessup was talking about. As the buggy followed the left-hand branch of the road through the curve toward the house, he ventured, "What is it exactly you want me to do about this party tonight?"

Jessup didn't seem put off by the question. "It's going to be up to you to keep my guests safe. There's going to be a lot of wealthy men up there tonight. I want enough armed guards around to protect them in case anyone tries to come in and hold them up."

"Like some of Conroy's cowboys again?" Longarm guessed.

Jessup gave a short bark of laughter. "I wouldn't put it past the man to try it!"

Longarm thought that was pretty unlikely. From everything he had heard, Conroy was a successful cattleman, and a rancher like that wasn't the sort to send his men out to raid a party of mine owners. Or to hold up a stage, for that matter. But he reminded himself that he didn't really know what was going on here, so he couldn't rule out any possibilities.

"Do you think you can find some trustworthy men to hire?" Jessup went on as he drove toward the house.

"I reckon I can," Longarm said with a nod. "I might talk to Salty. Since he's the regular driver on the stage run, he'll know most of the hombres around here. I trust him to steer me right."

"Yes, that's right, the two of you are old friends, aren't you? I've never gotten over how the West can be such a vast place, and yet at the same time it's a small world. It's certainly not unusual to run into people you've known elsewhere."

Longarm nodded. "*Es verdad*. That's the way border folks say something is true."

"You speak Spanish?"

"Some," Longarm said with a shrug. As a matter of fact, he could read and write Spanish fairly well, and he could understand it when it was spoken as long as the speaker didn't get to going too fast with the words.

"My wife tried to learn French and Italian. Had tutors and everything. But she never quite got the hang of it. Some things are just beyond Regina's considerable abilities, I suppose."

Longarm wouldn't know about that, since he didn't know Mrs. Jessup. All he really knew about her was that she had red hair . . .

Jessup drove up a circular path in front of the house and brought the buggy to a halt. He stepped down and tied the reins to an iron hitching post himself as Longarm got out of the buggy on the other side. Jessup led the way into the house.

A middle-aged Oriental man in a black suit met them in the foyer. He took Jessup's hat and said in unaccented English, "Good morning, sir. We missed you at breakfast."

"I worked most of the night in the office. Seemed easier just to catch a nap on the cot in the back room. Mrs. Jessup wasn't upset that I didn't come back last night, was she?"

"I wouldn't know, sir," the servant said. "She hasn't yet come down this morning."

"Sleeping in, eh? Well, that's fine. She needs her rest. Tonight will be a big night." Jessup turned to Longarm. "Come on, Parker. I'll show you the ballroom."

Their footsteps rang on the highly polished hardwood

floor as they went down a hall to a set of double doors. Jessup pulled both doors open and stepped through into a room that rivaled any Longarm had seen in the mansions of St. Louis or New Orleans. It was a huge, high-ceilinged chamber lit by a dozen crystal chandeliers, although the oil lamps in those chandeliers weren't burning at the moment. Curtains had been pulled back from several French doors along one wall to let in the morning sunlight. Most of the room was devoted to a dance floor, but there were also quite a few tables around the edges where guests could sit and drink and talk when they didn't feel like waltzing.

At the far end of the room was a stage where musicians could set up to play. Longarm wondered how Connie would feel about getting up there to sing for Jessup's party. That wasn't likely to happen, of course. Jessup wouldn't hire some saloon songbird to entertain his highfalutin' guests.

"Well, what do you think?" Jessup asked. "How many men will you need?"

Longarm did some quick figuring. He was no expert on such things, but protecting a bunch of rich folks while they attended a party was a matter of common sense more than anything else. A couple of men out front to keep an eye on the guests as they arrived, two or three more men armed with rifles to watch those French doors, a couple of men inside, including himself . . .

"Six ought to do it," he told Jessup. "They may need rifles, if they don't have their own."

"That won't be a problem. There's a whole rack full of brand-new Winchesters in my study. Are you sure that'll be enough men?"

"Well, I'll be here, too," Longarm pointed out. "That's seven well-armed men. Ought to be enough to make any desperadoes think twice about holding up the place."

"Hire a couple more so there'll be ten in all," Jessup said, his decisive tone brooking no argument.

"You're the boss," Longarm said. "I don't blame you for being careful, after losing all them gold shipments the way you have."

Jessup looked sharply at him. "What do you know about that?"

"Just what I read in the newspaper and heard around town. Seems like somebody's trying to break you by hitting your ore shipments. If that's the case, they sure might come after this party of yours, too."

Jessup gnawed on the unlit cigar for a second and then said, "That's exactly what I'm worried about, Parker. I've got enemies, and they'll stop at nothing to attack me."

"Most fellas who are successful in life have left some enemies along the way behind them."

Jessup gave another harsh bark of laughter. "I've left more than my share behind me, I suppose. But I'll beat 'em." One hand clenched into a fist. "They'll be sorry they came after Victor Jessup."

Longarm wasn't sure how he would have responded to that, but he didn't have to say anything because at that moment the Oriental butler appeared in the open doors of the ballroom and announced, "Sheriff Thacker is here to see you, Mr. Jessup."

Longarm tensed, wondering what was going to happen when the local law walked in and saw the very man he had been looking for earlier.

He sure hoped he didn't have to shoot his way out of here. A lot of lead flying around could wreak a heap of havoc on those fancy crystal chandeliers.

Chapter 6

Even if there had been some way for him to duck out of the ballroom without arousing suspicions, Longarm had no time to do such a thing. The sheriff entered the room hard on the heels of the butler, without waiting for Jessup to ask him to come in. He was a broad-shouldered man with a bit of a gut that showed he spent a lot of time behind a desk these days. He looked like he had been pretty active in his younger days, though. His face was weathered, and craggy eyebrows and a thick gray mustache dominated his features. He wore black wool trousers, a gray shirt, and a black vest and hat. An ivory-handled Colt was holstered on his hip.

"Morning, Mr. Jessup," he greeted the mine owner. "Getting ready for that big party tonight?"

"That's right, Sheriff," Jessup replied. "What can I do for you?"

"I just thought I'd stop by and see if there's anything you need, maybe some extra protection for your guests. The clerk down at your office said you'd come up here to your house."

Jessup shook his head, took the cigar from his mouth

and pointed it at Longarm. "Parker here is going to hire some guards and take care of that," he said.

It would have been all right with Longarm if Jessup hadn't drawn attention to him that way, but he had already noticed that the sheriff didn't seem to be interested in him. That was puzzling, of course, and it became even more so when the local lawman looked right at him without even a flicker of recognition.

"That so?" the sheriff murmured. He held out a hand. "Don't reckon we've met. I'm Sheriff Rip Thacker."

Longarm had already spent most of the morning confused as hell. He supposed there was no reason for this encounter to be any different. He shook hands with the sheriff and said, "Custis Parker."

"You're the gent who put those stage bandits to rout the other day, aren't you?"

Before Longarm could reply, Jessup said, "That's right. Saved our bacon, that's for sure."

Speculatively, Thacker looked Longarm up and down and then asked, "You ever think about carrying a badge, son? Might be able to find a place for you as a deputy."

"Parker works for me," Jessup said curtly. "He's not looking for a job."

Thacker shrugged. "Didn't figure it would do any harm to ask. You're sure there's nothing I can do for you, Mr. Jessup?"

"Not a thing."

"All right, then. Don't hesitate to call on me if you change your mind." Thacker nodded to Longarm. "So long, Parker."

He turned and walked out of the ballroom, leaving Longarm and Jessup standing there. Longarm couldn't draw any conclusion except that it hadn't been Thacker outside of his hotel room door earlier, after all.

But if that was the case, who had it been?

"I've got some work to do here," Jessup said once the

sheriff was gone. "I'll have Lee drive you back down to town in the buggy."

"No need," Longarm said. "It ain't so far that I can't walk."

"You're sure?"

"Yeah, it'll be fine."

"Then in that case," Jessup said, "I'll see you later, Parker. Perhaps you'd better be here with the guards you hire about an hour before dark, so that you can show them where they'll be posted."

Longarm nodded. "Fine by me. So long, Mr. Jessup."

Jessup went out of the ballroom by another door. Longarm used the one through which they had entered and walked back out into the main hall. He saw the Oriental butler, who he supposed was Lee, in the foyer by the front door, hanging a large, framed painting on the wall. As Longarm came closer, Lee looked over his shoulder at him, then nodded toward the painting and said, "Getting ready for tonight."

"Uh-huh," Longarm said. His heart slugged in his chest and he tried not to show the reaction he felt as he looked up at the painting. It was a portrait of Mr. and Mrs. Jessup. The mine owner sat in an ornately carved chair looking serious and dignified, and his wife stood slightly behind and to the side of him, her right hand resting on his left shoulder. She wore an elegant green gown, and the artist had done a good job of capturing the auburn highlights in the hair that was artfully arranged on her head. Her green eyes were compelling.

The last time Longarm had seen that auburn hair, it had been loose and in disarray, and those green eyes had been staring sightlessly at him. He had been hoping it would prove to be otherwise, but now there was no doubt.

The dead woman he'd woken up next to earlier that morning had been Regina Jessup.

• • •

The walk back down to Medallion's main street gave Longarm time to think. There had been no signs of a manhunt going on in the town earlier, and just now Sheriff Thacker sure hadn't acted like Longarm was wanted for murder or anything else.

Was it possible that whoever had busted into the hotel room hadn't been a lawman after all? Even though it seemed beyond belief, the events of the past hour or so indicated that no one had reported Mrs. Jessup's death.

And what about the hard case waiting in the alley to ambush Longarm? The only explanation that made any sense was that the gunman had been posted there to kill Longarm in case he woke up before the frame was complete and tried to escape. If Longarm had been gunned down in the alley and the hard case had testified that he had seen Longarm climb out of that hotel room window, the discovery of the dead woman would ensure that nobody would ask too many questions about who he was or what he was doing there.

Longarm's thoughts turned back to his missing credentials. Somebody knew he was a federal lawman and wanted to dispose of any threat he represented by stealing his bona fides and framing him for the murder of Regina Jessup. It seemed unlikely, though, that anyone would have killed Mrs. Jessup just to have a corpse to use in that frame-up. The killer must have wanted her dead, and placing the blame for the murder on Longarm was just an added bonus . . .

It was all too much for his brain to hash out, especially considering that there were facts in the case that he didn't know yet. But he hoped that talking to Salty would fill in some of the holes in his memory.

Since nobody seemed to be looking for him, he walked openly along the street to the stage line office. There was a large barn and corral out back, and he thought he might find Salty there. Sure enough, the old-timer was just coming out of the barn as Longarm strolled up.

"There you are," Salty said. "What'd the big boss man want?"

"You've heard about the party he's giving tonight?"

Salty stroked his beard. "Him and his wife, you mean?"

Regina Jessup wouldn't host any more soirees. But Salty didn't know about that yet, so Longarm just said, "Yeah."

"I heard about it."

"I'm responsible for hiring some guards and making sure nobody bothers all the rich, fancy guests."

Salty made a face and said, "Sounds like a plumb tiresome job."

Longarm didn't figure the party would ever take place, not with the hostess being dead and all. He said, "We need to palaver, Salty. I've got a problem, and I reckon you're about the only one in Medallion who can help me with it."

"Why in tarnation didn't you say so? I got me a cabin here in Medallion. The stage always lays over a night 'fore I start the run back to Kingman. We'll go to the cabin and have us a drink. You still partial to corn whiskey?"

"I never was. My druthers run to Maryland rye."

"Well, I ain't got none o' that."

"Corn whiskey it is, then," Longarm said.

The two men walked to the edge of town, where Salty pointed out a ramshackle old cabin that sat next to a small creek. "That's the place I call home when I'm up here," he said. "'Tain't much to look at it, but it's a roof over my head. Got a shack about like it down in Kingman, too."

"How'd you come to be driving a stage?" Longarm asked.

"Oh, I been a jehu a heap o' times in my life. I give up drivin' a freight wagon after that dust-up we was in a couple years back and drifted around for a spell. Then I sort o' lit here, by happenstance I reckon you could say, and the stage line was lookin' for a reg'lar driver. I took the job and been at it ever since."

"What do you know about Jessup?"

Salty shrugged. "He's rich. I reckon he figures that's all that matters."

"What do you think?"

"Well, he ain't a very friendly cuss, and he ain't got much patience, neither. Rides the folks who work for him pretty hard."

"I work for him," Longarm pointed out.

Salty grunted and said, "Jessup may think so. You an' me both know, though, that you work for Uncle Sam."

They reached the cabin and went inside. The place was as unprepossessing inside as out, but Longarm supposed Salty didn't need much in the way of creature comforts.

He sat down at the rough-hewn table while Salty got a jug and a couple of glasses from an orange crate that served as a cabinet. The old-timer splashed colorless liquid into the glasses and said, "Drink up."

As Longarm picked up his glass, he said, "You realize it ain't even noon yet, don't you?"

"I reckon it is somewhere," Salty pointed out. "I ain't prejudiced."

Longarm clinked his glass against Salty's and then threw back the whiskey. It burned going down and kindled an even hotter blaze in his belly. Longarm realized that he had just swallowed that fiery liquor on an empty stomach. There hadn't been any opportunity for him to eat, and besides, after waking up next to a dead woman, he hadn't had much of an appetite.

Still, he didn't need to get drunk, so he set his glass on the table and put his hand over it when Salty went to refill it. "One's my limit until we've had our talk."

"So talk already," Salty said. "You look a mite peaked, Custis. You feel all right?"

"Not really. I haven't felt very good since I woke up this morning."

"Too much Who-hit-John last night?" Salty asked with a grin. "Or was there a gal involved?"

"Too much of something," Longarm said grimly, "and there was a woman involved, all right. I wish there hadn't been."

"Why? Who was she?"

"Regina Jessup."

Salty's eyes widened in surprise. "Tarnation, Custis! She's married to one o' the richest, meanest fellers in the whole territory! I've heard rumors she's got a wanderin' eye, but still . . ."

"You ain't heard the worst of it. I woke up in bed with her this morning—"

"Lord have mercy!"

"And she was dead," Longarm continued. "Her throat was cut, ear to ear."

Salty just stared at him for a long moment, as if unable to comprehend what Longarm had just told him. Finally, in a hushed voice, he said, "Son . . . you didn't . . ."

"Of course I didn't," Longarm said. "But I reckon somebody wanted it to look like I did, and I don't have the slightest idea who or why. To tell you the truth, Salty, I ain't even sure why I'm here in Medallion. I could tell when I woke up that I'd been drugged, and now there are things I can't even remember."

"Yeah, I've heard that fellers are sometimes a mite addlepated after they've been slipped knockout drops." The old-timer poured himself another glass of whiskey and drank it straight down. "Tell me what you do know, and we'll try to figure this mess out."

"That's what I was hoping you'd say."

Quickly, Longarm filled Salty in on almost everything that had happened since he woke up that morning. He left out some of the details of his encounter with Connie

Maxwell, although he mentioned waiting in her room and the brief fight with the cowboy called Brice.

"Yeah, that'd be Brice MacPhail," Salty said. "Rides for Walt Conroy's Triangle C."

"I saw Conroy later," Longarm said. "At least, I think it was him. Tall, lean hombre with a gray mustache."

Salty nodded. "That's him."

"There was a girl with him," Longarm said, recalling the blonde he had taken for a man when she first rode into town. "Wore man's clothes and a six-gun."

"Yeah, that's Charlotte. She's Conroy's sister. Guess you don't recollect runnin' into her yesterday, do you?"

Longarm frowned. "Nope. You wouldn't think I'd forget something like that. She looked too young to be his sister, though. Conroy must be thirty years older than her."

"Yeah, but she's his half-sister," Salty explained. "Conroy's pa got married again when he was an old vinegarroon like me." Salty slapped the table and laughed. "Weren't too old to get his new young wife in the family way, though. Bad luck that the gal died when Charlotte was born. That left the old man to raise her, and when he passed on, Walt didn't have no choice but to take her in. She growed up wild as a mustang and twice as sassy. Ain't been nothin' but grief for Walt."

That was interesting, but Longarm couldn't see that it had anything to do with his problems. He said, "Anyway, Jessup doesn't seem to have any idea that his wife's dead, and the sheriff doesn't know about it, either. Or if they do know, they're mighty good at pretending they don't."

"Could've been somebody besides Rip Thacker who come bustin' into that hotel room. He's got a deppity name of Bardwell."

Longarm nodded. "I thought of that. I never got a good look at the gent."

"But why in blazes would anybody not say something if

they came in and found poor Mrs. Jessup like that, 'specially if it was Bardwell?"

"I don't know," Longarm said slowly, "unless whoever it was knew she would be in there."

Understanding dawned in Salty's eyes. "The feller who tried to frame you!"

Longarm nodded and said, "That's the way I've got it figured, at least for now. He was Johnny-on-the-spot, almost like he knew what he was going to find in there."

"And he had some gun-thrower waitin' out back in case you got away."

"Yep."

Salty tugged at his beard. "I reckon it all makes sense. Danged if I know *why* any of it happened, though."

"That's what I have to find out. And the first thing I want to know is what happened during this stagecoach robbery everybody says I broke up."

"You don't recollect what happened?" Salty asked with a frown.

"Not a bit of it," Longarm said. "It seems to me like I ought to, but . . . I just don't."

"Well, hell, lemme lubricate my throat a mite more, and I'll tell you all about it." Salty poured himself another drink, sipped some of the potent whiskey and smacked his lips. "That's mighty fine tonsil varnish."

"The holdup?" Longarm reminded him.

"Oh, yeah. It was thisaway."

The old-timer began to talk, and as Longarm listened to the cracked voice, he began to remember. . . .

Chapter 7

"Right there," Billy Vail said, stabbing a finger at the map on the wall of his office in Denver's federal building. He was indicating a spot in northwestern Arizona Territory. "That's Medallion."

Longarm stood up from the red leather chair in front of Vail's desk. Gray smoke curled from the tip of the cheroot clenched between his teeth as a long step took him over to Vail's side where he studied the map.

"Reckon I've heard of the place," he said, "but I don't think I've ever been there. Not that I recollect, anyway."

"It started out as a cattle town," Vail said as he went behind his desk and sat down. He motioned Longarm back into the red leather chair. The banjo clock on the wall ticked loudly. "A couple of years ago, though, gold and silver were found in the mountains just north of there. Several mines opened up and have been pretty successful. With the big cattle spreads south of town and the mines to the north, Medallion sits smack-dab in the middle."

Longarm nodded as he sat down again and cocked his right ankle on his left knee. "That can cause trouble."

"Yes, there have been reports of ruckuses between cowboys and miners." Vail picked up some papers on his desk. "That's not why I'm sending you there, though."

Longarm was patient. He knew Vail would get around to a full explanation in time. Anyway, he didn't have anything better to be doing at the moment than listening to his boss, whose rotund body, pink scalp and cherubic face obscured the fact that in his day he had been one of the hard-ridin'est, hell-roarin'est lawmen west of the Mississippi.

"The Oro Grande Mine has lost six ore shipments to robbers in the past few months," Vail went on. "That gold was ultimately bound for the mint here in Denver, so that makes it Uncle Sam's business. And ours."

Longarm nodded. "I figured that was where the trail was leading, Billy. You want me to find out who's responsible for those holdups and put a stop to them."

"That's right. You've done that sort of work before, Custis, and you're the best man for the job."

"Better be careful, Billy," Longarm advised wryly. "You go to talking like that, and I'm liable to take it as a compliment."

"Take it any way you damn well please, as long as you get the job done." Vail squared up the little stack of reports in front of him and passed them across the desk to Longarm. "You can read these on the train. Pick up your travel vouchers from Henry on your way out of the office."

Longarm rolled up the reports and stuck them inside his coat. They weren't his idea of light reading to pass the time while he was traveling, but he would study them anyway.

He blew a final smoke ring toward the banjo clock and got to his feet. "Is there a telegraph office in Medallion?" he asked.

"I doubt it."

"I'll let you know when I get to Kingman, then. Probably have to go the rest of the way by stagecoach or horseback."

Vail held out his hand. "Good luck, Custis. I reckon this is the sort of job you can just about do in your sleep, though, so you may not need much luck."

Longarm grinned, shook hands with his boss, and said, "A fella always needs luck, Billy. Even when he's sleeping . . ."

After getting his travel vouchers from Henry, the four-eyed young clerk who played the typewriter in the chief marshal's outer office, Longarm went back to his rented room on the other side of Cherry Creek, packed a bag and made the train just as it pulled out for Santa Fe, Albuquerque, and points west.

After Longarm spent an uncomfortable night of sleeping sitting up, the train pulled in to Kingman, Arizona Territory, the next morning. Longarm disembarked, sent the promised wire to Billy Vail to let the chief marshal know he had arrived, then walked over to the stage line office to discover that he had missed the coach for Medallion by less than an hour. There wouldn't be another one for two days.

Longarm didn't want to wait that long, so he walked on down the street to a livery stable and rented a horse and outfit. The animal was a sturdy-looking buckskin with a temper. Longarm learned quickly not to turn his back on the critter, or else he'd run the risk of having the horse take a nip out of his backside.

Since he was going to be riding up to Medallion, he borrowed the livery stable tack room to change clothes in, taking off his brown tweed suit, silk vest, white shirt and string tie. He stowed the garb in his saddlebags, along with the big turnip watch with the .41 caliber derringer attached to it by an innocuous-looking watch chain.

In place of the town clothes he donned range gear: denim trousers and jacket and a butternut shirt. When he rode out of Kingman, he might have been taken for a drifting cowpoke rather than a lawman. That was just the way he wanted it.

Among the papers Billy Vail had given to him was a small map showing this part of Arizona Territory, and Longarm had studied it enough during the train ride so that he had no trouble finding the trail to Medallion. He kept the buckskin moving at a brisk pace as he rode northwest.

By late afternoon he had covered a lot of ground and was riding through a semiarid stretch of terrain dotted by sagebrush and cut by ridges and gullies. From high ground he could see the more fertile rangeland sweeping off to both east and west.

The sudden popping of gunshots in the distance made him rein in sharply and sit up straighter in the saddle. He heard a heavy boom that he took to be a shotgun discharging. Somebody was in trouble up ahead, not too far away by the sound of it, and Longarm knew that even if he hadn't been a lawman, his nature wouldn't have allowed him to ignore the fracas. He heeled the buckskin into a run.

The trail swept around a cluster of boulders. Longarm saw that it cut through a ridge ahead of him. Steep banks rose on both sides of the trail, forming a fairly narrow passage. That passage had been blocked by a large rock shoved down from one of the banks. With that barrier in its way, the stagecoach that ran from Kingman to Medallion wasn't able to get through.

Longarm saw puffs of smoke from the ridge and knew right away that bandits were responsible for blocking the trail and stopping the stagecoach. They had probably opened fire as soon as the coach lurched to a stop. He looked for the driver, wondering if the man had already been gunned down.

The greener roared again as it was fired from underneath the stage. The driver and the shotgun guard, if there was one, must have taken refuge under there when the bullets began to fly. A series of sharp cracks from inside the

56

coach told Longarm that at least one of the passengers was fighting back, too. Pinned down like they were, though, they didn't have much of a chance.

Not unless he took a hand and evened the odds a little. He pulled his Winchester from the sheath strapped under the saddle flank and worked the lever, jacking a round into the chamber. As he brought the rifle to his shoulder, Longarm saw a man move up on the ridge. The hombre was trying to change position so that he would have a better angle to fire down at the trapped coach, but what he really accomplished was to put himself right in Longarm's sights. The big lawman instantly squeezed the trigger.

In the brief glimpse he had gotten of the holdup man before he fired, Longarm realized that the outlaw wore a long duster and had a hood of some sort pulled over his head, under a jammed-down Stetson. The mask, which had eye-holes cut into it, completely concealed his face otherwise.

The Winchester blasted and kicked against Longarm's shoulder. He saw the robber knocked into a spinning fall by the bullet. Longarm worked the lever again as one of the other bandits, dressed the same way in duster and hood, leaped into the open to hurry over to his wounded comrade. Longarm fired again and saw the second man clutch at his leg and stumble. The owlhoot stayed on his feet and managed to bring his rifle around and return Longarm's fire. Longarm yanked the buckskin to the side of the trail as he heard the wind-rip of a slug passing close by his ear.

After slapping his horse on the rump to send it trotting back out of the line of fire, Longarm knelt behind one of the boulders that littered the ground on both sides of the trail. He had thirteen rounds left in the Winchester, and he quickly sprayed half a dozen of them among the hidden bandits, three shots on each side of the bluff. Their hiding places concealed them from the people in the coach, but not from Longarm. His bullets sent them scurrying for cover. The shotgun blasted again from down below when one of the outlaws darted out from behind a rock. Longarm heard the faint yell of pain as buckshot peppered the man. He heard someone else shout, "Let's get the hell out of here!"

Longarm threw out a couple of shots to hurry them on their way. A few moments later he heard the urgent rataplan of hoofbeats from both sides of the ridge and knew the gang was fleeing. Still, he waited where he was for a couple of minutes to make sure they weren't going to double back and open fire again.

When the hoofbeats faded away and he was convinced the owlhoots were really gone, he stood up and called, "Hello, you in the coach! Reckon it's safe for you folks to come out now!"

He saw a lone man crawl out from under the coach. Just a driver, then, no shotgun guard, Longarm told himself. Surprisingly, the man seemed familiar.

Longarm walked back along the trail to where his rented horse had stopped. All the shooting had spooked the buckskin a little, but the animal calmed down as Longarm spoke to it in a soft, soothing voice. He got hold of the reins, swung up into the saddle and rode along the trail toward the coach, where the passengers had now disembarked.

As Longarm rode up, he got a better look at the driver, and a shock of recognition went through him as he recognized the old jehu. "Salty!" he exclaimed.

The bearded man looked up at him and said, "Well, I'll be a horned toad's uncle! Custis, is that you?"

Longarm dismounted and gripped the gnarled paw that the old-timer thrust out at him. He hadn't seen Salty since a case of his a couple of years earlier down Yuma way had had them fighting outlaws side by side. "It's good to see you again, you old pelican!" he said.

Four passengers had climbed down from the stage. Cheap suits and pasty complexions marked two of them as traveling salesmen. Longarm pretty much ignored the drummers and looked at the other two, a man and a woman, both of whom were well-dressed. The man was in his forties, the woman probably around fifteen years younger. But from the possessive way the man kept his arm around her, Longarm thought it likely he was her husband.

She was a looker, sure enough, with dark red hair and a richly curved body that her gray traveling outfit couldn't completely conceal. Boldness lurked in her green eyes as she looked at Longarm.

The man extended his hand. "Seems like you came along just in time to save us from being robbed and maybe murdered," he said. "You have my thanks. I'm Victor Jessup."

The name rang plenty of bells in Longarm's brain. According to the reports Billy Vail had given him, Victor Jessup was the owner of the Oro Grande Mine. It was his gold shipments that had been stolen half a dozen times in recent months.

Longarm shook hands with him and said, "Howdy. My name's Parker. Front handle is Custis."

He shot a glance at Salty. The stage driver knew good and well that Longarm's real name was Custis Long. He knew as well that Longarm was a deputy United States marshal. Longarm hoped that Salty was quick enough on the uptake to realize that he didn't want Jessup to know who he really was.

Of course, there wouldn't have been anything wrong with telling Jessup his real identity. After all, he had come to Arizona Territory to put a stop to the problems plaguing Jessup's mining operation.

But Longarm had found over the years that many times he could uncover the information he needed to know easier and quicker if no one was aware that a federal lawman was poking around. He would tell Jessup the truth sooner or later, but for now he would prefer to remain undercover.

Salty didn't say anything, and Jessup didn't seem to have noticed the glance that passed between Longarm and

59

the jehu. Jessup released Longarm's hand and went on, "This is my wife."

Longarm tugged on the brim of his hat as he nodded to her. "Ma'am. Honored to make your acquaintance."

She put out a gloved hand to shake hands like a man. "I'm Regina Jessup," she said coolly. "I'm pleased to meet you, Mr. Parker. Doubly so because you ran off those highwaymen."

"Owlhoots rub me the wrong way," Longarm said.

"Why is that?" Jessup asked. "Are you a lawman?"

"Nope, just a drifter," Longarm lied. "On my way to a place called Medallion. I thought I might be able to scare up some work there."

Briskly, Jessup said, "You most certainly can. I'll hire you myself. I own the Oro Grande Mining Company, which is headquartered in Medallion."

Longarm frowned slightly. "I ain't sure I'd make much of a hand as a miner."

"A man of your talents would be wasted in a mine shaft," Jessup said. "There's been trouble recently, and I had more in mind to hire you as a bodyguard and troubleshooter."

Salty spoke up, saying, "That there's a fine idea, Mr. Jessup. I've knowed ol' Custis for a long time, and he's a ring-tailed roarer when he gets a-goin'. If you got trouble, he'll sure shoot it for you."

Longarm's eyes narrowed. "Don't run too big a windy there, old son."

Jessup laughed and said, "No, I have a feeling he's right. What do you say, Parker? Since you're on your way to Medallion anyway, why not arrive there with a job already in hand?"

Longarm's hesitation was just for show. So far, things couldn't have worked out much better. He had managed to gain Jessup's gratitude and confidence without even having to reveal who he really was.

After a moment, Longarm nodded and said, "All right, you've got a deal." They shook hands again.

"Excellent," Jessup said. "Now, I suppose if we're ever going to reach Medallion, we'd better start giving some thought to moving that rock out of the trail."

"It'll be a chore," Salty warned.

Jessup removed his coat and hat and handed them to his wife. Longarm saw that Jessup wore a shoulder holster containing a pistol, probably a .38 or a .36. He must have been the one firing at the outlaws during the brief shootout.

The mine owner started to roll up his sleeves and motioned peremptorily for the two drummers to do likewise. "A little hard work never hurt anybody," he said. "Let's get started. We're not going to reach Medallion before nightfall as it is."

"Nope, we'll have to lay over 'til mornin' at the Cottonwood station a couple o' miles from here," Salty agreed. "We'll be doin' good to get that boulder moved and get that far before dark."

Longarm started toward the big rock in the trail with the other men. Mrs. Jessup stopped him by laying a hand on his arm. "Would you like for me to hold your hat, too, Mr. Parker?" she asked.

"No, ma'am, I reckon that's all right," he told her.

That hadn't been the question she was really asking, though, Longarm figured as he joined the other men in putting his shoulder against the boulder and heaving against it.

The bold look in Regina Jessup's eyes had made it plain she was interested in holding more than just Longarm's hat.

Chapter 8

As Salty had predicted, it took some time and quite a bit of sweating and groaning before the boulder was rolled far enough to the side of the trail so that the stagecoach could squeeze past it. Once that was done, the passengers climbed back inside the coach. Longarm tied the buckskin on at the back and climbed to the driver's seat next to Salty. This would give him a chance to talk to the old-timer in private. No one inside would be able to hear them over the hoofbeats of the team and the rattle of the wheels.

"I reckon you must be workin' undercover," Salty said when he had the coach rolling along briskly.

"That's right," Longarm said. "I'm obliged to you for not giving away who I really am."

Salty snorted. "Figured you must have a good reason, otherwise you wouldn't be doin' it."

"My boss sent me down here to find out who's been holding up Jessup's ore shipments."

Salty let out a low whistle. "Yeah, the Oro Grande's sure enough been havin' trouble gettin' the gold and silver down to Kingman. Been some guards been shot up pretty bad, too. Couple of 'em have even died."

"I'm sorry to hear that. I aim to do my best to put a stop to it."

"Ain't nobody better suited to the job than you, Custis."

"What can you tell me about Jessup?"

"He ain't no shrinkin' violet," Salty said with a shrug. "Drives hisself hard, and ever'body else, too. Comes from back East somewheres, but I've heard him talkin' about workin' in coal mines and steel mills when he was young, so I reckon he's a pretty tough hombre."

"Got himself a young, pretty wife," Longarm commented.

Salty glanced over at him. "That he does," the old-timer agreed. "I seem to recollect that you got an eye for a pretty woman yourself, Custis. Might not be a good idea to go sniffin' around Mrs. Jessup, though."

"I don't intend to," Longarm declared. "I was lucky to come along when I did so I could bust up that robbery and get on Jessup's good side. I don't aim to ruin that by going after his wife."

"Well, it's a rare thing for any man to think with his brain 'stead o' his pecker, so I reckon we can mark this down as a red-letter day!"

Longarm grinned at the old pelican's gibe, but he grew solemn again as he asked, "What can you tell me about those ore shipments that have gone astray?"

"All I know is what I've heard around Medallion. After the first couple o' shipments got hit, Jessup and his mine manager started tryin' to cross up the thieves by shippin' at odd times and havin' the wagons follow different routes than usual. Nothin' worked, though. They still had just about ever' other shipment hit by bandits."

"The local law hasn't had any luck trailing the thieves?"

"Sheriff Thacker took out a posse ever' time there was a holdup, but they always lost the trail."

"What do you think about the sheriff?"

"Rip Thacker's all right, I reckon," Salty said. "Wouldn't

be surprised if he's seen his best days as a lawman, though. He ain't as eager as he once was to track down lawbreakers."

Longarm thought it over for a minute and then asked, "Is there any chance Sheriff Thacker is in on the holdups? Could he be working with the gang pulling them?"

Salty took one hand off the reins and used it to scratch his beard. After pondering Longarm's question, he said, "I don't reckon a fella can ever really rule out anything until he knows for sure, but Thacker don't strike me as a crook. I could be wrong, though. I sure ain't sayin' he's pure as the driven snow, neither."

"I've heard that there's been trouble between the miners and the cowboys from the spreads to the south."

Salty's head bobbed up and down. "Damn right there has been. I reckon most cowpokes hate a sheepherder worse'n anything else, but they ain't overfond o' miners, neither. I've heard about quite a few fights they've had in the saloons and whorehouses and gamblin' dens in Medallion."

"Any chance some wild young cowboys are behind the robberies of those ore shipments?"

"There's always a chance. Most o' the ranchers try to ride herd on their crews, but hell, they don't like the miners, neither, and Jessup is the big auger amongst the mine owners."

"What it sounds to me like," said Longarm dryly, "is that I'm liable to run into trouble just about any which way I turn in Medallion."

"Yep." Salty nodded solemnly. "That there's just about the size of it."

He drove on toward Cottonwood Station, explaining that the stopover was about three-fourths of the way between Kingman and Medallion. It was just too far to make the run in one day, unless the stagecoach got an early start and nothing happened to delay it. That happened sometimes, but neither of those things was true on this day.

Longarm rode with his Winchester across his knees, keeping an eye out for any sign of trouble. He didn't think those desperadoes would try to stop the stage again after the way he had peppered them with lead, but there was no guarantee of that. He wondered, too, if the same bunch might be responsible for the ore shipment holdups. It certainly seemed possible.

Cottonwood Station consisted of a squat log building, an adobe barn and a pole corral where fresh horses for the stagecoach teams were kept. Longarm had seen plenty of way stations just like it in his travels. As Salty brought the coach to a halt in front of the log building at dusk, a tall, gaunt man with bristling chin whiskers and a black patch over his left eye stepped out to greet them with an upraised hand. "Howdy, Salty," he called. "Expected you earlier."

"We got held up, Ezra," Salty responded.

The station keeper frowned. "You mean delayed, or really held up?"

"Some o' both. A gang o' owlhoots blocked Buzzard Bait Cut and threw down on us when I reined in. We might've been buzzard bait for real if Custis here hadn't come along when he did." Salty inclined his head toward Longarm as he spoke.

Ezra grunted. "Yeah, I was wonderin' who your guard was."

"This is Custis Parker, an old pard of mine. He ain't workin' for the stage line. He just happened to ride up when we needed him."

"Pleased to meet you, Parker," Ezra said. "Well, climb on down from there, fellas. I'll have the boys unhitch the team."

Several Mexican hostlers had come out of the barn. At Ezra's orders, they began taking the harnesses off the horses attached to the stagecoach. Salty climbed down from one side of the box while Longarm dropped lithely to the ground from the other side.

Salty opened the door of the coach and announced, "Cottonwood Station, folks. We'll lay over here tonight and get an early start in the mornin' with a fresh team. Ought to get us into Medallion 'fore noon."

Jessup stepped out of the coach first and turned back to help his wife climb down. The two salesmen followed her.

"Sorry the accommodations ain't fancy, folks," Ezra said to Jessup and Regina.

"As long as you have a decent place for my wife to sleep, that's all that matters," Jessup said.

"Yes, sir, we'll make her as comfortable as we can."

Ezra led the four passengers into the station. Longarm and Salty hung back to watch the hostlers finish the job of unhitching the team and taking the horses to the corral, where they were turned in with the other horses.

"I don't know that Miz Jessup's ever stayed in a place like this," Salty said quietly. "Ever' time she's rid with me before, we've been able to make the run without stoppin' over."

"She'll be all right," Longarm told him. "I've got a feeling she's one lady who can make herself at home wherever she is."

"Hope so. I don't want Jessup raisin' holy ned with the line on account of how his wife was treated."

Longarm unsaddled his horse and put the buckskin in the corral, too. By then Salty was satisfied that the hostlers had done a satisfactory job of caring for the stagecoach team. He and Longarm went into the station. Salty carried his shotgun, and Longarm had the Winchester tucked under his arm.

The station wasn't any fancier on the inside than it was outside, with plain log walls and a rough puncheon floor. A massive stone fireplace took up almost one entire wall. A long table with benches sat near the fireplace. Several mounted heads of bighorn sheep, elk and deer adorned the walls. On the far side of the room, a crude wall partitioned off a sleeping room where female passengers could spend the night. Men had to make do with bedrolls and cots in the main room.

The building was sturdily constructed, though, and Longarm was willing to bet that it was warm in the winter. In the summer, such as now, the thick walls kept it from becoming too stifling. He had stayed in worse places; that was for sure.

Judging from the expression on Regina Jessup's face as she sat at the table, she wasn't impressed by the station. Chances were, she *hadn't* stayed in worse places, although Longarm realized he couldn't know that about her. He didn't know where she came from or what her background was.

A small fire burned in the fireplace, with a pot of stew simmering over it. The room was also lit by several oil lamps that hung from the ceiling. The aroma that emanated from the big black cast-iron pot reminded Longarm that it had been quite a while since he'd eaten.

Ezra was getting ready to start dishing out bowls of stew. The two drummers sat at the far end of the table from Mrs. Jessup, maintaining a respectable distance from the lady. One of them had taken out a pipe, filled it with tobacco and lit it. The other was smoking a cigar, the same sort of cheap, three-for-a-nickel cheroot that Longarm favored. Jessup sat beside his wife, a much more expensive cigar in his mouth.

Longarm and Salty went to the table and sat down about midway along its length, placing the shotgun and the Winchester on the floor at their feet. Jessup looked at them and asked, "Is it necessary to bring those weapons to the dinner table with you?"

It was a stretch to call this rough-hewn piece of furniture a dinner table, but Longarm knew what he meant. Salty said, "Just bein' cautious, Mr. Jessup. There's owlhoots in these parts. We know that from experience. And you can't never tell when some band o' renegade 'Paches will decide to raise a little hell." He nodded to Mrs. Jessup. "Beggin' your pardon for the language, ma'am."

She didn't say anything, just gave him a weak smile.

Ezra brought the first two bowls of stew to the Jessups. "Here you go, folks. Eat hearty."

Jessup dug in with an appetite. Regina was content to pick at her food. She kept shooting glances toward Longarm from the corners of her eyes. He tried to act like he didn't see them.

The stew tasted as good as it smelled, Longarm discovered when Ezra brought bowls to him and Salty. He thought the meat was elk, but he wasn't sure about that. There were thick, savory chunks of it, along with potatoes and carrots and wild onions, and that was all that mattered. Washed down with steaming cups of strong black Arbuckle's coffee, it was a meal fit for a king. Well, a cattle king, maybe. Longarm had eaten plenty of meals like this in his younger days, when he was working on the trail drives up from Texas to the railhead in Kansas.

Jessup said to Salty, "You don't think we'll have any trouble reaching Medallion before midday tomorrow?"

"No, sir, I don't. Not unless somethin' mighty unforeseen happens."

"Good. I need to get up to my mine and go over several things with the superintendent, and Mrs. Jessup and I are planning to give a small party for some of our friends at our house in Medallion."

"I'm sure it'll be a mighty fine affair, ma'am," Salty said in an attempt at some rough gallantry.

"Well, I'll do the best I can," Regina said. "There's only so much a hostess can do in such surroundings."

Jessup frowned slightly, and Longarm figured he didn't care for his wife putting on airs that way. What else could he expect, though, from a rich, beautiful woman who had probably been raised with the proverbial silver spoon in her mouth?

After dinner, Regina retired rather quickly to the privacy of the partitioned-off sleeping room. The men sat around smoking and talking for a while, and then they turned in as well. Ezra blew out the lamps and let the fire burn down to glowing embers.

Longarm waited for sleep to claim him, but it didn't. A restlessness grew inside him instead. After lying there and listening to Salty Ezra, and the two drummers sawing wood for a while, he got up and slipped outside, thinking that maybe some fresh air and another cheroot would settle him down enough so that he could sleep.

He walked out to the corral to check on the horses. They were all calm, letting him know that there weren't any mountain lions lurking around the area. The scent of big cat would spook a horse about as fast as anything. More snoring came from inside the barn, where the hostlers slept.

The night air was cool and crisp at this altitude, even during the summer. Longarm breathed in a lungful of it and then turned sharply, his hand flashing to the butt of his gun as a foot scraped on the ground behind him.

Chapter 9

"Oh my goodness!" Regina Jessup said as she took a hurried step backward and raised her hands in front of her. "Don't shoot, Mr. Parker. It's only me."

Longarm relaxed a little and took his hand off the Colt. He growled, "No offense, ma'am, but what in blazes are you doing out here?"

"I couldn't sleep," she said with a defiant toss of her head. Her auburn hair was loose now and fell around her shoulders in thick, dark waves in the moonlight. The silvery glow revealed as well that she wore some sort of loose sleeping gown. She had to be a little chilly in it.

She continued, "There's nothing wrong with me being out here, is there? Or do you think some of those renegade Apaches our driver spoke of might be around?"

"I don't think you got to worry about Apaches tonight," Longarm said. "But there could be snakes around, not to mention other kinds of varmints."

"Then it's a good thing you're out here, too, isn't it, so that you can protect me," she said with a trace of mockery in her voice.

"I don't know. Could be I'm one of those other kind of varmints you've got to look out for."

She laughed. "Don't worry about me, Mr. Parker. When it comes to male varmints, I can take care of myself."

Longarm bet that was right.

Still, he didn't think it was a good idea for Regina Jessup to be wandering around like this. He said, "If your husband wakes up and realizes you ain't in your room, he's liable to be worried."

She moved a step closer to him and said, "For one thing, Victor is a very sound sleeper. Once he dozes off, nothing short of a dynamite blast will disturb him for hours. For another, even if he was awake, why would he know that I'm not in my room?"

"Well, he might come to, uh, pay you a visit," Longarm said.

"You mean he might be interested in having conjugal relations with me?" Regina laughed. "Victor is very particular about when and where and how such things take place. It wouldn't even occur to him at a stagecoach station in the middle of nowhere."

"Maybe not, but it'd still be better if you went back inside, ma'am," Longarm persisted. "You've got a reputation to think of and all."

"You think I care about that?" Suddenly she was very close to him, so close that he could feel the heat of her body coming through the thin gown she wore. "You think I care about anything except doing this?"

Her arms went around his neck and pulled his face down to hers as her body surged against him, molding itself to his. He felt every rich, unfettered curve of her through the gown. Her lips pressed hotly, hungrily, against his.

Longarm had kissed married women before. He had even bedded a few of them, when the circumstances were just right. But most of the time it went against the grain for him. He didn't dwell on it, but his ma back in West-by-God Virginia had raised him to be a gentleman, and that was just the way he lived without thinking about it.

Regina Jessup was a beautiful woman, no doubt about that. Longarm's hands instinctively caressed her ripe, ready body. Her kiss held an undeniable passion and an urgency that roused a fever inside him. He cupped one of her breasts, filling his hand with the warm, firm globe of female flesh. His thumb found the erect nipple and stroked it through the fabric of her gown.

She brought one hand down from his neck and pressed it against the hardness at his groin. He couldn't tell her that he didn't want her. That would be an obvious lie.

But wanting and actually doing were two different things, and Longarm knew this wasn't right. The fact that Regina Jessup wasn't happy with her marriage didn't give her the right to go out and prowl around like some sort of she-cat. Or maybe it did, but not with him. He moved his hands to her shoulders and gently pressed her back a step.

"This ain't a good idea," he told her.

She gave his shaft a squeeze through his trousers. "I think it's a very good idea," she breathed. "From the feel of this, you do, too."

"A fella's, uh, male equipment ofttimes has a mind of its own, ma'am."

"Are you trying to tell me that you *don't* want me?"

"I ain't saying that. I just think it'd be a good idea if you went back inside and didn't say nothing about this to your husband."

"Don't worry, I don't intend to tell him." She leaned into him again, flattening her breasts against his chest. Her lips caressed the strong line of his jaw, planting kisses there and on his throat. She caught hold of his hands and brought them to the swell of her hips. "It won't hurt a thing. What we do won't really matter."

"No, ma'am, I reckon it won't," Longarm said. "That's why we hadn't ought to do it."

She pulled her head back and looked up at him. "Who the hell are you," she demanded, "some damn fairy-tale

73

knight on a white charger? I'm going to pull my gown up and lean against this wall, and you're going to get behind me and take me, do you understand? Take me as hard and as fast and as rough as you want."

"I don't reckon so," Longarm said slowly.

"Why not, damn you! Do you think you're too good for me, cowboy?"

"Nope. I just figure it's not the right thing to do."

"You supercilious bastard!" Her hand flashed up, aiming a hard slap at Longarm's face.

The blow never landed. Longarm didn't seem to move all that fast, but he reached up and grabbed her wrist before she could slap him. When she lashed out at him with her other hand, he caught that wrist, too, and held her there. She writhed against him, but there was nothing sensuous or exciting about her movements now. She was furious, practically spitting at him like that she-cat he had thought of her as a few moments earlier.

"Settle down," he told her, squeezing her wrists hard enough to get her attention without really hurting her. "You made a mistake. Chalk it up as that and go on. Ain't any shame in it."

"I . . . I'll tell my husband you attacked me!" she panted.

"I can't stop you from saying anything you want to say. Whether or not he believes you . . . well, that's up to him."

"You're the one who's making a mistake." Suddenly, she stopped struggling. Her body went soft and pliant against his. "I'll do anything you want. If you want something different, I don't mind. You can do anything you want to me. And I'll do anything you want me to do to you. Just tell me what you want."

"I want you to go back in the station and get some sleep," Longarm said. "Morning will be here before you know it, and it'll be time to head on in to Medallion."

She slipped her wrists out of his now-loosened grip and

stepped back. A hollow laugh came from her. "Go back inside and go to sleep," she said. "That's what you want me to do. But it's easier said than done. You don't know what it's like to have this ache inside you, this terrible emptiness that can't be filled. You don't know how desperate I am for . . . for . . . something . . . ."

She broke off with a soft cry and turned away from him. Unsteady footsteps took her back toward the station.

Longarm watched her go. He knew about longing. He knew about desperation and loneliness. Everybody who was human had felt those things at one time or another. It was part of being alive.

He hoped that somewhere, somehow, Regina Jessup would find what she was looking for.

But all he knew for certain was that she wasn't going to find it with him.

Regina was surly the next morning, but her husband didn't appear to notice that much difference in her attitude. She avoided Longarm, not speaking to him or even looking at him. That was just fine with him.

Salty took note of the change. While he and Longarm were watching the hostlers hitch a fresh team to the stagecoach, the old jehu commented quietly, "Miz Jessup don't seem near as taken with you today, Custis. Somethin' happen last night?"

"Nothing worth talking about," Longarm said.

"All right, but I'm glad we ain't got far to go today. That gal's so mad about somethin', it makes the air around her turn plumb chilly."

The sun hadn't been up long when the passengers got into the stage and Longarm and Salty climbed to the driver's box. Salty took up the reins while Longarm sat beside him, Winchester in hand. The buckskin was tied on to the back of the coach again.

Ezra had fortified them with a breakfast of flapjacks,

75

bacon and more Arbuckle's. As a rule, the food that Longarm had encountered at most stage line way stations was terrible. The fare that Ezra dished out was a very welcome exception to that rule.

Salty whipped up the team, shouted to the horses and got the coach rolling. It rocked easily along the trail. As they rode, Salty pointed out the mountains to the north and explained that the settlement of Medallion was located at the base of them, just beyond the good cattle range.

The rest of the trip was uneventful. There were no more holdup attempts. The stage road entered Medallion from the south, merging with the main street. Another fork of the road curved up to a big, impressive mansion overlooking the settlement.

Salty nodded toward it and said, "That's the Jessup house. They got a place up at the Oro Grande, too. That's the name o' the mine Jessup owns. And there's a house in Kingman for when they're down there. Ownin' three houses is a mite gaudy, to my way o' thinkin'."

"Not if you spend some time in all three places, I reckon," Longarm said.

"Well, maybe not. Still, I never knowed anybody else who had three houses."

Neither had Longarm. Victor Jessup had to be making a lot of money off the Oro Grande mine. That stream of riches was threatened, though, by whoever was masterminding those ore shipment robberies.

Medallion was a good-looking town. It had grown to a respectable size as a supply point for the ranches to the south. Once silver and gold had been discovered in the mountains to the north, that had made the settlement develop even more.

Salty brought the coach to a halt in front of the stage line office. A barn and corral were out back. A man in a suit and a bowler hat sat on a bench in front of the office, as if he were waiting for the arrival of the stage. If he was a passenger, though, he didn't have any bags with him, Long-arm noted.

The man wasn't a passenger. He stood up and waited until Salty had climbed down and opened the coach door. Then, as Jessup stepped down, the man said heartily, "Good morning, Mr. Jessup! Welcome back. Any comment for the *Weekly Medallion*?"

"No, I don't have anything to say," Jessup replied curtly. The man in the bowler hat didn't seem offended by the tone of Jessup's response.

Jessup helped Regina down from the coach, and she said, "I have a comment, Mr. Brandstett."

The man, who obviously put out the local newspaper, poised a stub of pencil over a pad of paper he took from his pocket. "Of course, Mrs. Jessup," he said eagerly. "What would you like to tell the citizens of Medallion?"

"Victor and I are going to be having a grand ball for all our friends," Regina said. "It will be the highlight of the social season in Medallion."

Longarm had climbed down from the driver's box. He leaned a shoulder against the boot at the rear of the coach and put an unlit cheroot in his mouth. The Winchester was tucked under his arm.

He smiled wryly as he listened to Regina. He had a feeling it wouldn't take much for a party to be the highlight of the social season in Medallion. While the settlement had a little polish about it, for the most part it was still a rough-and-tumble frontier town, without much need of, or patience for, fanciness and folderol.

"That sounds wonderful, ma'am," Brandstett said. "Is the public invited?"

"Well, no," Regina admitted. "Attendance will be by invitation only. But we expect all the other mine owners and their families, as well as the superintendents and their families, and perhaps even some important visitors from Kingman and Flagstaff."

"Oh." Brandstett's face had fallen a little when Regina said that the party would be a private affair. That wasn't quite as newsworthy as something that the whole town would be invited to. But he put a smile back on his face as he went on, "I'm sure it will be the most exciting thing Medallion has ever seen."

"And we'll want *you* there, of course, so that you can report on it for your newspaper," Regina went on with a smile.

"Oh!" Brandstett brightened up considerably at that. "Certainly! Thank you, Mrs. Jessup. I'll be there, you have my assurance of that."

Jessup looked impatient, and Longarm figured he'd had enough of standing there listening to his wife and Brandstett go on about the party. He looked down the street and then said, "Here comes Lee with the buggy. Let's get our bags, Regina."

"The stage line has someone to handle that, Victor," Regina said coolly.

That was true enough. The man who ran the stage line office in Medallion had emerged from the building, followed by a couple of husky local boys. The youngsters took several large trunks and carpetbags from the boot and loaded them into the back of the buggy that pulled up a moment later with an impassive-faced Oriental in a dark suit at the reins.

Jessup stepped over to Longarm and said, "Come up to my house this afternoon, Parker. We'll talk about that job I have for you."

Longarm nodded. "All right, Mr. Jessup. Anything you want me to do between now and then?"

"No. You might want to get a hotel room, since you're going to be around here for a while. Need an advance on your wages?"

"Nope, I'm all right for now." Longarm didn't intend to actually take any money from Jessup if he could avoid it.

He didn't mind pretending to work for the man, but he didn't want to accept wages from him.

Jessup and Regina got into the buggy. The Oriental servant swung it around and drove off toward the big house that seemed to be visible from just about anywhere in the settlement.

"What are you gonna do now, Custis?" Salty asked.

"You heard the man," Longarm replied. "I figured I'd go see about renting a room in the hotel."

"That can wait." Salty wiped the back of his hand across his mouth. "It's been a long, dusty trail, and I could sure use somethin' to cut that dust. Come along with me and have a drink."

That sounded like a pretty good idea to Longarm. He stepped up onto the boardwalk, turned to accompany Salty and ran smack-dab into a man who was going the other way.

Chapter 10

The collision wasn't hard enough to knock either man off his feet. Longarm stepped back and said, "Sorry, mister. I didn't see you in time."

The man was tall and angular, with dark hair under a pushed-back hat. A tin star was pinned to his red plaid shirt, and a walnut-butted gun hung holstered at his right hip. He frowned as he said, "Better watch where you're goin', friend."

"Said I was sorry," Longarm responded. He started to move past the lawman. Whenever he was working on a case, he tried to cooperate with the local star-packers, even when he was undercover and they didn't know he worked for Uncle Sam.

The man put a hand on Longarm's chest to stop him. "Sorry ain't good enough."

Salty said quickly, "Uh, Deputy, this here is a friend of mine, name of Custis Parker."

"You'd better tell your friend to be more careful, old man."

Longarm kept a tight rein on his temper. It would be easy for him to get angry with this deputy, but it wouldn't accomplish anything. He said in a deceptively mild tone, "I ain't looking for trouble, Deputy . . . ?"

"Bardwell," the man snapped. "Dave Bardwell."

"Well, Deputy Bardwell, like I said, I ain't looking for trouble, just a drink and maybe something to eat and then a hotel room."

"Staying around Medallion for long, Parker?" Bardwell made it sound like that wouldn't be a very good idea.

"I reckon that depends on Mr. Jessup. He's the one I'm working for."

That made a difference. The arrogant glower on Deputy Bardwell's face disappeared. He said, "You mean Mr. Victor Jessup?"

"One and the same," Longarm said.

Salty let out a cackle of laughter. "You should'a seen it, Deputy. A gang o' road agents had us pinned down at Buzzard Bait Cut, but then ol' Custis came along and made 'em hightail it. Some o' the best shootin' I ever seen in all my borned days."

"Wait a minute," Bardwell said. "Somebody tried to rob the stage?"

"That's right. And Mr. an' Miz Jessup was on it, too. Could' a been mighty bad if Custis hadn't come along when he did."

Bardwell looked at Longarm with an expression of grudging respect. "I reckon the community owes you some thanks, then," he said. "Mr. Jessup means a lot to Medallion."

Jessup's *money* meant a lot to Medallion, that was what Bardwell meant, thought Longarm. If anything was to happen to Jessup and the Oro Grande closed down, it would be a bad blow to the settlement.

"I'm just glad I came along in time to help out," Longarm said. "Now, if you'll excuse us, Deputy . . ."

"Yeah, go ahead." Bardwell added as an afterthought,

"The Cattle King's the best saloon in town, if you're lookin' for a drink."

"That's where we was headed," Salty said.

They walked on down the street. Longarm felt Dave Bardwell's eyes boring into his back. Quietly, he said, "That fella didn't exactly take a liking to me."

Salty chuckled. "Bardwell's a prickly sort of gent, sure enough."

"What sort of lawman is he?"

The old-timer shrugged his shoulders. "He's good at breakin' up saloon fights and handlin' proddy cowpokes. That's about all Sheriff Thacker asks him to do."

Longarm hadn't met the sheriff yet, of course, but if Deputy Bardwell was an example of the local law, he figured he couldn't expect much help from them. That was all right with Longarm. He was used to playing a lone hand.

The Cattle King Saloon was a big place. It took up half a block. The batwinged entrance was on the corner. Even at this hour—it wasn't quite noon yet—Longarm heard piano music coming from inside the saloon before he and Salty reached the entrance.

The batwings swung open, and for the second time in just a few minutes, Longarm bumped into somebody else. It was a more pleasant accident this time, at least for him. The young woman who had just run into him stepped back and said, "Oh!"

She was tall and lithe and had a coltish look about her. Though she was dressed like a man, in a faded blue work shirt and jeans, the clothes hugged her body tightly enough to reveal its curves. A broad-brimmed Stetson hung behind her head by its chin strap, and blond hair fell around her shoulders and down her back. Longarm figured she was around twenty years old.

"Beg your pardon, ma'am," he said.

"Hell, no need to beg my pardon," the young woman

said bluntly. "I'm the one who ran into you, mister. Are you all right?"

"I reckon I ain't damaged," Longarm said dryly.

The young woman stepped around him and went on her way. Salty watched her go, his gaze lingering on the sway of her rounded rump. He sighed.

"I'd like to know why it is that pretty gals never run into me," he complained. "I may be old, but I'd still enjoy havin' 'em bump up against me ever' now and then."

"I didn't hear you grousing when that deputy plowed into me," Longarm pointed out.

"Well, I don't want that. Ain't you payin' attention?"

Longarm aimed a thumb at the batwings. "Let's go get that drink. Maybe they've got a free lunch in here, too."

"Oh, they do. A mighty fine one, at that."

Salty was right. One end of a long bar inside the saloon was filled with platters of ham and roast and biscuits. There was gravy and molasses, too, and a big bowl of boiled eggs. Longarm and Salty went to the bar and got themselves a mug of beer each, then hit the free lunch and carried plates of food over to a table where they sat down.

The meal was good, and as Longarm ate and washed it down with sips of beer, he looked around the saloon. There were two bars, one on each side of the room, with plenty of tables between them. One area was set aside for gambling. There were poker tables covered with green baize, a faro layout and a roulette wheel. At the far end of the room was an elevated stage with a purple velvet curtain pulled across it.

Longarm nodded toward the stage and asked, "Do they put on shows in here, too?"

"Yep. Some o' the girls who work here dance a mite, and they got a gal singer, too. I never heard her myself, but folks say she sings real pretty. I know she's a looker. I seen her around a time or two."

"Maybe I'll get to take in a show while I'm here."

"Might be worth your while." Salty snorted. "Just stand around for a while. I'm sure that songbird'll run plumb into you, like Charlotte Conroy just did."

"That's the blonde out on the boardwalk?"

"Yeah. Her brother Walt owns the Triangle C, the biggest cattle spread hereabouts."

Pitching his voice low, Longarm said, "That'd be one of the fellas who's had trouble with Jessup, right?"

"Well, the gents who work for Jessup and Conroy have had a few ruckuses, that's for sure. The two of 'em ain't ever taken a swing at each other personal-like, as far as I know."

The idea that Conroy, or some of his men, might be behind the robberies of the ore shipments was still just a theory, of course, but it was one that Longarm would have to look into while he was here.

They finished their lunch and drank another beer, and then Longarm said, "Point me to the hotel, and I'll go see about getting a room."

"You can't miss it. It's right next door. I got a little cabin down by the crick and you'd be welcome to stay with me, Custis, but there ain't much room."

"That's all right," Longarm told the old-timer with a smile. "I like to have plenty of expenses so the clerk in Billy Vail's office back in Denver will have plenty to fuss about when I get back." He came to his feet. "I'll see you later."

"I'll be around. Stage don't pull out again for a while."

Longarm went next door to the hotel, which was called the Horton House. He got a room on the second floor and went up to leave his war bag and Winchester lying on the bed. Then he walked back to the stage line office to check on his horse. The buckskin had been unsaddled and turned in to the corral with the animals from the team. The station manager assured Longarm it would be all right to leave the horse there while he was in Medallion.

"Any friend of Salty's is welcome to a favor or two," the man said. "He's one of the most dependable drivers we have."

"He's a good man, all right," Longarm agreed.

With that taken care of, he strolled around Medallion for a while, just looking over the settlement and getting familiar with it. He saw Deputy Bardwell again, standing on the opposite boardwalk and giving him a speculative look, but Longarm ignored the lawman and moved on.

Around midafternoon, after saying good-bye to Salty as the stage pulled out on the return run to Kingman, Longarm turned his steps toward the Jessup house. It was a pretty good walk up to the place, but it didn't seem worth going to the trouble of getting his horse from the stage station corral and saddling the buckskin just to ride that far. Back in his cowboying days, he had shared the usual horseman's disdain for walking anywhere. Over his years as a lawman, though, he had come not to mind it so much.

When he reached the house, he paused for a moment to look at the well-tended lawn and the flower beds and the tall, straight pine trees on either side of the porch. The house itself was a big, hulking thing, not particularly attractive, but the surroundings were pretty. Longarm went to the front door and used the lion's-head knocker to announce himself.

The Oriental servant he had seen earlier in town answered the knock. "Mr. Parker," the man murmured. "Mr. Jessup told me to expect you this afternoon. Please come in. May I take your hat?"

Longarm took off his Stetson and said, "I'll hang on to it, if that's all right."

"Certainly. Follow me, sir."

The servant led Longarm to a big room that appeared to be a study, library and office combined. Victor Jessup sat behind a large desk that was cluttered with papers.

"Glad you showed up, Parker," he greeted Longarm.

"Regina and I will be leaving shortly for the Oro Grande. Be back tomorrow sometime. How does a hundred a month sound?"

The sudden switch in topics took Longarm by surprise. "For wages, you mean?"

"Exactly." Obviously, Jessup believed in plain talk and not wasting time.

Longarm nodded and said, "That'll be fine. What do I do for that hundred?"

Jessup picked up a smoldering cigar from an ashtray and put it between his teeth. "Whatever I tell you to do."

Longarm's jaw tightened a little. He didn't like Jessup, but the role he was playing required him to go along with the man.

"All right. What's that going to be?"

"To start with, I want you to poke around town and see if you can find out anything about those ore shipments I've had hijacked." Jessup pushed some papers across the desk. "Here's the details of the robberies, as well as I've been able to reconstruct them. Study those reports. Ask questions. Hell, I don't know. If you find out *anything,* you'll be doing better than Sheriff Thacker and that deputy of his."

Longarm picked up the papers. Again, luck was riding with him. He had come to Medallion to investigate the ore shipment robberies, and here was Jessup cooperating with him without even knowing that Longarm was a federal lawman.

"I'll see what I can find out," he said.

"Good. If I get back in time tomorrow I'll talk to you about the party. It'll be two nights from now."

Longarm's eyebrows rose. "I'm invited?"

"You'll be making sure that no one tries to hold up my guests." Jessup's teeth clenched harder on the cigar. "That attack on the stagecoach yesterday made me more convinced than ever that someone has a personal grudge against me. I think the same men who have been stealing my shipments were the ones who ambushed us. The ones who got the gold were masked, too. I wouldn't put it past them to strike at me again during the party."

What Jessup said made sense. Longarm said, "You must have an idea of who's behind all the trouble."

Jessup clenched a fist. "Walt Conroy. That's what I think. But I can't prove it. You might start your job by looking into the activities of Conroy and his men."

"All right," Longarm said. If Jessup was right, it wouldn't be the first time that a simple feud had escalated into robbery and murder attempts.

"That's all," Jessup said. "I'll see you tomorrow or the next day."

"You don't want me to go up to the mine with you, just in case somebody tries to bushwhack you again?"

Jessup shook his head. "Several armed guards who work at the mine are coming down to accompany Regina and me back up there. They should be here any minute."

Longarm nodded. Jessup began studying some of the other papers and making notations on them, so Longarm took the reports the mine owner had given him and left the room. The placid-faced servant was waiting outside to show him to the door.

When he was outside and headed back down to the settlement, Longarm breathed a little sigh of relief. He had hoped that he wouldn't run into Regina Jessup while he was there, and good fortune had smiled on him.

Since Jessup was convinced that Walt Conroy had something to do with his troubles, and since that sounded like a plausible theory to Longarm, the next logical step was to pay a visit to the Triangle C. Longarm got the buckskin from the stage station corral, slapped his saddle on the horse, and rode out of town, heading back down into the cattle ranges to the south of Medallion. He had talked to

Salty enough during the ride up here to know the direction to the Conroy ranch headquarters.

He was several miles out of town when the sudden crack of a rifle made him sit up straighter in the saddle and wonder what the hell was going to happen now.

Chapter 11

The first shot was followed by a flurry of several more. Judging by the sound of the reports, they came from both rifles and handguns, meaning several people were involved in the fracas. With a sigh, Longarm heeled the buckskin into a run. He couldn't just ignore a small-scale war like the one that seemed to be going on somewhere ahead of him.

He followed the shots to a red sandstone bluff that jutted up from a flat, grassy stretch of ground. Some large sandstone boulders littered the ground at the base of the bluff where they had fallen from the rimrock in ages past. A cloud of gunsmoke hung over those rocks, and as Longarm came into view he saw another spurt of smoke add to the haze as somebody holed up in there let off a round.

Whoever had taken shelter in the rocks was firing toward a line of trees about fifty yards away. As Longarm reined in, well off to the side behind some brush, he saw answering puffs of smoke from gunmen using the trees for cover. They kept up a rapid, rolling barrage of fire that must have had the man in the rocks hugging the ground to avoid all the flying lead.

The hombre managed a return shot every once in a while, but that wasn't doing much good. As long as the men in the trees kept him pinned down, sooner or later they would pick him off, or a ricochet would get him.

Grim lines appeared on Longarm's face as he watched the shoot-out. Even without knowing who was forted up in those rocks, he felt a surge of sympathy for the poor son of a bitch. It rubbed him the wrong way to see half a dozen men ganging up on one lone hombre, no matter what the circumstances.

A moment later, the situation became even more urgent, because sunlight suddenly flashed on long blond hair as the defender in the rocks shifted position. Longarm leaned forward in the saddle. There might be more than one person in these parts with long blond hair, but Longarm had a feeling that was Charlotte Conroy trapped in there.

He swung down from the saddle and tied the buckskin's reins to a bush. Then he pulled the Winchester from its sheath and started circling carefully behind the trees where the gunmen lurked as they poured lead toward the rocks.

At least six men were firing from the trees. Longarm hoped he could take them down one at a time without the others realizing what was going on. If he could, he might be able to pull Charlotte out of this fix.

That would certainly make him more welcome on the Triangle C, and he could turn that to his advantage in his investigation of the ore shipment robberies. However, the most important thing at the moment was saving Charlotte's life.

A horse's nicker caught his attention, and he dropped into a crouch as he worked his way through some undergrowth. He came in sight of seven horses being held by one man. Longarm's breath hissed between clenched teeth as he saw that the man wore a long duster and a flour-sack hood with eyeholes cut out of it. A high-crowned hat was crammed down tight on the man's head, holding the hood in place.

Thoughts flashed through Longarm's brain. Unless there were *two* gangs of owlhoots around here who wore dusters and masks—pretty damned unlikely in his opinion—these were the same men who had stopped the stage the day before. Now for some reason they were trying to kill Charlotte Conroy.

Victor Jessup had been convinced that Walt Conroy and the Triangle C were to blame for everything bad that had happened to him, from the ore shipment robberies to the attempted stage holdup. But that made no sense. Conroy's men wouldn't be trying to ventilate their boss's sister.

Longarm knew he would have to hash it all out later. For now, he edged through the brush toward the man holding the horses.

The gunfire had the animals spooked, and one of them suddenly tossed his head and pulled his reins loose from the outlaw's hand. The man turned swiftly and made a grab for the trailing reins, and that brought him face-to-face with Longarm. With a startled yelp, he forgot about the horse and reached for the gun on his hip instead.

Longarm lunged forward and lashed out, clouting the masked hombre over the head with the barrel of the Winchester. The man's tall hat blunted the force of the blow somewhat, so that he was stunned but not knocked down and out. Longarm grabbed his wrist while the man's six-gun was just partway out of the holster. He didn't want any shooting to alert the others that something was going on behind them. He put a shoulder in the man's midsection and they both went down, with Longarm landing on top.

The fall made him drop the Winchester, so he used a fist instead and slammed it into the man's face. The flour-sack hood concealed the man's features but didn't stop the punch from landing cleanly. His head bounced hard off the rocky ground and he went limp.

Longarm plucked the man's gun from its holster and

tossed it away in the brush. He pulled the hood off, revealing the coarse, unshaven features of a typical owlhoot. Longarm had never seen him before.

He yanked the man's belt loose, rolled him over and used the belt to bind his hands behind his back. Then he wadded up the hood and stuffed it in the outlaw's mouth.

The man was starting to regain consciousness as Longarm stood up, but all he could do was make some muffled, outraged squawks as he thrashed around. The other men wouldn't be able to hear those sounds over the roar of guns.

Longarm picked up his Winchester and said, "You got a choice, old son. You can lay there and take your chances, or you can try to yell and get away and make me use this rifle butt to stove in your skull. It's up to you."

The man's struggles subsided. He had no way of knowing that this tall, dangerous-looking fella was a lawman and wouldn't kill him in cold blood.

Longarm held up a finger and said, "Smart move." Then he catfooted toward the other men who were still firing at Charlotte Conroy.

They didn't know it yet, but they had been set a-foot. Their horses had all taken off when Longarm tackled the man who had been holding them.

Longarm came up behind one of the men, who crouched behind a tree and fired an old Henry rifle toward the rocks, spacing out his shots evenly. A hard butt stroke to the back of the head with the Winchester sent the hooded man slumping to the ground, unconscious. Longarm knew the man wouldn't wake up for a while, so he didn't take the time to tie this hombre's hands.

He worked his way to the side, searching for the next man. The sound of shots brought him to a duster-clad fella who knelt behind the trunk of a fallen tree.

Some instinct must have warned the gunman, because he turned suddenly toward Longarm, his hand filled with a long-barreled Remington. Longarm had to throw himself desperately to the side as smoke and flame geysered from the barrel of the heavy revolver.

Caution had to go by the wayside in favor of survival. Longarm fired the Winchester as he fell to the ground. When he landed he rolled over, jacking the rifle's lever as he did so. He came to a stop on his belly, ready to fire again if he had to.

A second shot wasn't needed. His first bullet had driven fatally into the gunman's chest, driving him backward over the log. He was draped there now, the front of his shirt sodden with blood under the duster, his arms hanging loosely at his sides. His hat had fallen off because his head was thrown so far back.

Longarm leaped to his feet. He didn't know if the exchange of shots would warn the other men that there was an enemy in their midst, but he'd had an idea. He peeled the hood off the dead man, then slung him to the ground and quickly took the duster off him as well. Longarm had never seen this gent before, either. He was cut from the same cloth as the other one.

There was no blood on the duster or the hood. Longarm donned the long coat, then lifted his hat and pulled the hood over his head. He stuck his own hat under the duster and put it on.

Then he broke into a run through the trees, heading toward the other men.

He came in sight of them a moment later and croaked, "The horses! Some bastard's after the horses!"

The four men broke off their firing and turned to hurry toward him.

Longarm was counting on the hood to disguise his voice enough to be unrecognizable as he went on harshly, "There's a bunch of riders comin', too! We'd better get outta here!"

"What about that damned girl?" one of the other gunmen bleated.

"She never saw our faces," another man snapped. "That's probably some of Conroy's punchers comin'! Let's go!"

They broke into a run toward the spot where they had left the horses. Longarm lagged behind, and as soon as he got a chance he ducked away from them, darting into a little brushy gully. Charlotte Conroy was still firing from the rocks, and an occasional bullet zipped through the trees. If the other men missed him, they would probably think that he had been hit and fallen without them noticing.

Longarm cast aside the hood and duster he had taken from the man he'd killed and waited until the sound of hoofbeats told him the outlaws had caught their horses and hightailed it without waiting to see if a force of enemy gunmen was really approaching. He climbed up out of the gully and made his way toward the place where the outlaws had left their horses.

Along the way he passed the spot where he had left the unconscious gunman. The man was nowhere to be seen. He must have regained his senses in time to see his comrades fleeing and had gone with them. The one Longarm had left tied up wasn't where he had been, either. The others must have freed him and taken him with them.

He made his way through the trees to the edge of the open ground in front of the bluff. When he got there, he had to duck as a bullet smacked into a tree trunk close beside his head. The shot came from the rocks. "Hold your fire!" he shouted. "I'm a friend! Don't shoot!"

"Friend, hell!" a clear female voice came back, confirming for Longarm that the person holed up in the rocks was really Charlotte Conroy. "You're one of them!"

"No, I ain't! I'll step out and prove it!" Longarm took a deep breath and stepped into the open so that Charlotte could get a good look at him. He held the rifle in one hand over his head and had the other hand upraised, too.

"That don't prove a damn thing!" she shouted back at him. "You just took off your duster and hood!"

"Nope, those old boys lit a shuck out of here. I fooled 'em into thinking that a bunch of your brother's cowboys were riding this way."

For the first time the girl sounded a little doubtful about his identity as she called, "You know Walt?"

"I know of him, just like I've heard about you, Miss Conroy! Fact of the matter is, you and me bumped into each other in Medallion earlier today, outside the Cattle King Saloon!"

"Son of a bitch! I thought you looked familiar, mister!" Charlotte stood up, rifle in hand, and trained the weapon on him unwaveringly. "Come on over here, but don't try anything funny!"

"That's the furthest thing from my mind, ma'am," he assured her.

He tucked the Winchester under his arm and then approached her, keeping his hands in plain sight the whole way. She moved out from the rocks to meet him.

As she did, her right leg suddenly buckled and threatened to go out from under her. She caught herself with an effort. The strain visible on her pale face told Longarm she was in pain. He saw a dark, spreading stain on the leg of her trousers.

"You're hit, aren't you, Miss Conroy?"

Tight-lipped, she replied, "It's just a scratch. And there's not a damned thing wrong with my trigger finger."

"I've had some experience patching up bullet wounds. I'd be glad to take a look at that one."

"I'll just bet you would," she said sharply. "Who are you?"

"Name's Custis Parker." He took a chance that she wouldn't have heard about him saving the stagecoach from the outlaws and then going to work for Victor Jessup. "I'm

97

just a grub-line rider. Was on my way out to your brother's spread to see if he might be hiring."

"That was pretty slick work, outwitting those rustlers . . . that is, if you really did. I'm still not convinced that you're not working with them."

"Rustlers, you say?"

"That's right. I caught them trying to push a jag of Triangle C cows off our range. They came after me. I guess they didn't want any witnesses around."

So the same gang robbed ore shipments from the Oro Grande, held up stagecoaches, and now rustled cows, too? They were a busy bunch of varmints.

"I don't have anything to do with rustlers," Longarm assured her. "I can prove it. I'll take you back to your brother's headquarters. Where's your horse?"

She inclined her head toward the rocks and said grimly, "Back there. Dead. He stopped a bullet while those bastards were chasing me. He got me as far as the rocks before he gave out. If he'd gone down while we were still out in the open, I wouldn't have had a chance."

That was likely right. Longarm said, "My buckskin can carry double for a ways. How far is it to the Triangle C ranch house?"

"About five miles."

Longarm looked at the sky and nodded. It was late afternoon, but he thought they could make it that far before dark.

"I'll go get my horse and come back here. That is, if you trust me out of your sight, ma'am."

"Stop ma'aming me, blast it. I ain't no high-toned lady."

Maybe not, but she was a beauty, even dirty, blood-stained and powder-grimed.

"I'll go with you," she went on, taking a step forward. She had lowered the rifle, but it was still pointed in Longarm's general direction.

Suddenly, her eyes rolled up in her head and her face

grew even paler. She lurched to the side as her wounded leg buckled again. With a choked exclamation of "Oh, hell!" she dropped the rifle and fell.

Longarm sprang forward to catch her before she could hit the ground. The way her head lolled loosely on her neck told him that she had passed out. She must have lost more blood than he had realized. Or it was possible she was hit somewhere else and he hadn't noticed that wound yet.

They weren't going anywhere until he tended to her and found out just how bad a shape she was in. She might be too injured to travel even the relatively short distance to the Triangle C headquarters.

Lifting her in his arms, he carried her back into the cluster of boulders. She was a big, solid girl, but Longarm was able to handle her without much trouble. He avoided the place where her dead horse lay and found another spot where he could lower her gently to a sandy, relatively soft stretch of ground.

Then he set about taking her clothes off, chuckling to himself as he thought that the circumstances sure as blazes could have been a lot better for doing a thing like that.

Chapter 12

He didn't have to remove Charlotte Conroy's shirt because he was able to check well enough to see that she hadn't been wounded above the waist without doing that. The trousers had to come off, though, and as Longarm unbuttoned them and peeled them down over her hips and thighs, he discovered that evidently Charlotte didn't believe in wearing anything under them. He had expected some bloomers or at least the bottoms from a pair of long underwear.

It wasn't gentlemanly to gawk at a gal while she was unconscious and in such a vulnerable position. So he steadfastly averted his eyes from the triangle of thick, luxuriant hair that was just a trifle darker than the hair on her head and concentrated instead on the wound on her right thigh.

A bullet had plowed a shallow groove through the outer part of her thigh, knocking out a chunk of meat in the process. It was a messy, painful wound, but not a life-threatening one unless it festered, and Longarm intended to see to it that that didn't happen.

There was a canteen strapped to his saddle. With some water from it and a rag he took from his saddlebags he swabbed away as much of the blood as he could. Then he took a small silver flask from his saddlebags and uncorked it. After taking a nip of the Maryland rye in the flask, he poured the rest of it over the wound. Charlotte Conroy shifted around and groaned, feeling the pain of the fiery liquor in the wound even though she was unconscious.

When he was satisfied that he had cleaned the wound the best he could, Longarm took one of his clean shirts and ripped it up for bandages, tying the strips of cloth as tightly as he could around Charlotte's thigh without cutting off the circulation to the rest of her leg. Finally, he was finished and knew that he had done everything possible for her.

Not quite everything, he reminded himself. He picked up her trousers. The right leg from the thigh down was soaked with blood, as well as having a ragged tear in it where the bullet had struck it. Longarm took his clasp knife from his pocket and opened it, then used the keen blade to slice off the trouser leg just above where the bloodstain started.

He got the trousers back on her and buttoned them up just before she regained consciousness. Charlotte stirred again and her eyelids flickered open. She stared up at him uncomprehendingly for a moment, and then she tried to sit up. She failed and fell back with a moan.

"Take it easy," Longarm told her. "You lost a heap of blood from that leg wound, so I ain't surprised your head's a mite dizzy. Just lay there and rest."

She closed her eyes and threw an arm over her face. "How . . . how bad is it?" she asked.

"Not that bad," Longarm assured her. "Like you said, it's just a scratch. Pretty deep one, though. I cleaned it up and bandaged it. You stay off that leg and let it heal, and you ought to be good as new in a couple of weeks."

"I don't *have* a couple of weeks! I've got to get back to the ranch and tell Walt about those damned rustlers."

"Later," Longarm said. "I could put you on my horse,

but if you passed out and fell off, you might do even more damage to that hurt leg of yours. Might break your other leg or an arm. Just give it a little time, and I'll see to it you get back to the Triangle C."

Charlotte sighed. "We're on Triangle C range right now. Maybe one of the crew will come along, and we can send him back to the ranch house for a wagon."

"That'd be a stroke of luck, all right. I'd go myself, but I ain't sure it'd be a good idea to leave you here alone. Those masked men could double-back and cause more trouble. I don't think they will, but we can't know that for sure."

She moved her arm and opened her eyes to look up at him. "What did you say your name was?"

"Custis Parker, ma'am."

"I told you about that ma'am stuff."

He smiled. "So you did. I'll just call you Miss Conroy, I reckon."

"Oh, Lord, that's worse! Makes me sound like some prissy little bitch. My name's Charlotte, but that ain't much better. Call me Charlie."

"I don't reckon I've ever run into anybody named Charlie who was quite so pretty," Longarm said.

"Pshaw! You might as well hush up with that horse hockey. It don't work with me." She raised her head enough to look down at her legs. "Did you take my pants off me, or did you just cut off that right leg?"

Longarm supposed he could have lied about it, but he generally told the truth whenever it was possible. "I took your trousers off," he said. "I wanted to see if you were hit anywhere else."

She gave an unladylike snort. "Yeah, I'll bet that was all you wanted to see."

"I was more concerned with patching up that wound than anything else," Longarm said.

Charlotte—or Charlie, as she wanted to be called—didn't look convinced, but she didn't press the issue. Instead she sighed and said, "I reckon I ought to thank you. I'd probably be a goner by now if you hadn't come along. I was hoping I could hold out against them until it got dark, then I was gonna try to slip away. Chances are they'd have picked me off before then, though."

Longarm glanced up at the sky. "Seeing as it ain't dark yet, you're probably right. Why don't you tell me what happened?"

"Like I said before, I came upon those rustlers while they were trying to drive off some Triangle C cows. I can see now that what I should have done was to hang back and follow them, so I could find out where they were going."

"But that ain't what you did, I reckon?"

"No, I hauled out my long gun and let fly at the bastards. Nobody steals our cows and gets away with it, least of all a bunch of damn rock-eaters!"

Longarm frowned. "You think those men were miners?"

"Of course I do. You ain't been around these parts long, have you?"

"Just got here today."

"Well, if you'd been here for a while you'd know that the fella who owns the Oro Grande mine and the men who work for him are behind all the troubles we've got."

"From what I heard in town, it sounds like the Oro Grande's got troubles of its own. Something about some ore shipments being held up."

Charlie shook her head. "I wouldn't put it past those bastards to be lying about that, just to keep folks from being suspicious of them."

"Those fellas who were trying to shoot you didn't look like miners to me."

"Anybody can put on a duster and a mask," Charlie said scornfully.

Longarm couldn't argue with that. And as he thought about it, he had to wonder if Charlie might be on to something. He couldn't figure out what motive Victor Jessup would have for faking the ore shipment robberies, though. He couldn't accept Charlie's theory that it might be for appearance' sake. For the time being, he put the idea aside, although he would keep his eyes open for any evidence that might point in that direction.

He steered the conversation back to the rustling by asking, "What happened to those Triangle C cows you saw being wide-looped?"

Charlie shook her head. "I don't know. I imagine they're on the way to wherever the rustlers were taking them. The bunch split up, and some of them came after me while the rest kept pushing the cows."

"So you got yourself shot and didn't keep the cattle from being swiped."

She frowned, balled a hand into a fist and punched him on the leg as he sat beside her. "You don't have to make me sound like such a damn fool."

"Maybe caution just ain't in your nature."

"That's right. It ain't. What business is that of yours?"

"Not a bit," Longarm said with a shake of his head. "I imagine it's a mite frustrating to that brother of yours, though."

"Walt's my brother. He ain't my pa. What I do or don't do ain't any of his business, no matter what he thinks." With a glare, Charlie turned her head and looked in the other direction.

Longarm pushed himself to his feet and said, "I ought to go get my horse. You'll still be here when I come back, won't you?"

"I don't think I'd get very far hobblin' on one leg, do you?" Charlie answered in a tone of disgust.

Longarm took a cheroot from his shirt pocket and put it in his mouth as he walked away. He grinned around the tightly rolled cylinder of tobacco. Charlie Conroy had a feisty way about her, that was for sure. He wouldn't have put it past her to crawl all the way back to the ranch house, if she took a mind to.

He found the buckskin where he'd left the horse and untied the reins. A few minutes later, when he led the horse back to the rocks at the base of the bluff, he saw that Charlie had scooted herself over some so that she could sit up with her back braced against one of the rocks. She had her rifle lying across her legs.

"I feel better now," she announced. "Not so dizzy. But I don't know if I'm up to riding."

"We can wait here until you're ready," Longarm said.

"It'll be dark in less than an hour. You'd better gather some wood, build a fire and fix us some supper."

Evidently they were going to spend the night here. Longarm hadn't planned on that, so he hadn't brought along any supplies. "I don't have anything to cook," he said. "Might scare up a few strips of jerky out of my saddlebags."

Charlie sighed. "Well, that'll be better than nothing, I suppose. We'll need that fire anyway. It gets chilly out here at night, even in the summer."

"Yes, ma'am . . . I mean, Charlie."

He was busy for a while, gathering some branches from under the trees where the outlaws had taken shelter and then building a small fire so that the heat from it would radiate against the rocks and keep him and Charlie warm.

She had an opinion about most things, from the way he built the fire to the way he unsaddled the buckskin, and she didn't mind expressing them. Longarm didn't take offense . . . but he did things how he wanted to, whether Charlie agreed with it or not.

"You are one hell of an irritating man," she said after a while.

"So I've been told. I sleep good at night, though, so my conscience must be clear."

"Where's that jerky you said you had?"

106

"Comin' up."

They sat on opposite sides of the fire and gnawed on the tough strips of meat, washing the jerky down with sips of water from Longarm's canteen. He had used all the Maryland rye he'd had left in the flask to clean the wound on her thigh. Probably a good thing, he told himself, since neither of them needed to get tipsy out here.

The air cooled off quickly once the sun was down. "I told you it would get chilly," Charlie said.

"So you did. You need a blanket?"

"I could use one . . . especially since you cut half my trousers off. *After* you had them off me and did God knows what to me while I was out colder'n a mackerel."

"All I did was clean and bandage that bullet graze."

Charlie looked like she didn't believe that for a second.

Longarm got a blanket from his saddlebags and spread it over her. She patted the ground next to her and said, "Sit with me."

Longarm lowered himself to the sandy ground, close to Charlie but not quite touching her. He said, "You reckon we ought to start for your brother's ranch house once you've warmed up a mite?"

"I don't know. I'm not sure I can ride yet."

"I can see where it would be painful to sit a saddle with a bullet-gouged leg."

Charlie slid down until she lay on her side, facing away from Longarm. "I think I'll rest a while."

"All right. I'll keep watch."

His Winchester was beside him. He let the fire burn down until it was just red embers glowing in the darkness. Charlie's breathing grew deeper and more regular, and he knew she had gone to sleep.

Time passed as night settled down fully on the Arizona countryside. Longarm thought about the case. He hadn't made much progress, but he knew a few things. He would keep poking around and see what else he could find out.

Charlie didn't stay asleep for very long. After a while she stirred a little and said quietly, "Custis?"

"Yeah?"

"I know I'm a bitch sometimes. I ain't easy to get along with."

"Shucks, I hardly noticed," Longarm said with a chuckle.

"I do appreciate the way you helped me. And . . . and I'm glad you're here with me tonight."

He rested a hand on her shoulder for a second and said, "So am I."

"You reckon you could . . . lay down here beside me?"

"I don't know if that would be a very good idea," Longarm said slowly.

"I do. I think it'd be a fine idea."

"You sure about that?"

"You ever know me *not* to be sure about something?"

He had to chuckle at that. "I've only known you a few hours."

"That's long enough."

Longarm didn't argue with her any more. He stretched out beside her. "Under the blanket," she whispered. He pulled the blanket over him, and she scooted back, snuggling against him spoon-fashion.

It was inevitable that he would feel a reaction to having a warm round female rump tucked up against his groin like that. As his shaft hardened, she felt it, too, and she began to move her hips slowly and sensuously.

"Careful of that wounded leg," Longarm cautioned her.

"It doesn't hurt at all now."

"You don't want it to start bleeding again, though."

Charlie lifted her hips enough to shove her mutilated trousers down over them. Longarm wondered when she had unfastened the buttons. He didn't spend a lot of time pondering the question, though. He ran a hand over the smooth curves that were now bared to him. His hand slipped between her legs and found the heated wetness at her core.

She groaned in passion and said in a voice husky with desire, "I want you, Custis. Take me."

"I'll have to be careful—"

"The hell with that! My leg's fine, I tell you!"

Longarm didn't want to argue with her. He leaned closer to her and kissed her on the neck instead. Then his lips grazed her ear and the line of her jaw. She turned her head and his mouth found hers.

The kiss lasted only a moment. Then Charlie shifted to bring herself even closer to Longarm and said, "Please."

Longarm unbuttoned his trousers and worked them down enough to free his shaft. Charlie's legs parted welcomingly as the long, thick pole of male flesh pushed between them. He found the opening to her femininity and surged forward as she thrust back to meet him.

She cried out softly as he sheathed himself fully within her. He put his arms around her and held her steady as he drove in and out in a patient, deliberate rhythm. Despite her plea to ignore her injured leg, he couldn't do that. He was as careful as his own mounting arousal would allow him to be.

Charlie's breathing increased. Longarm slid a hand down to her breasts and cupped the right one through her shirt, stroking the erect nipple with his thumb. His manhood delved deeper and deeper in her until she began to spasm around him.

That brought Longarm to the brink, too, and he didn't try to hold back. He exploded inside her, flooding her with his seed as culmination swept over both of them.

He was breathing hard by now, too. He held her close and felt her heart hammering under his hand. His own heart was galloping at a pretty good pace. Slowly, their racing pulses eased. Longarm's now softening shaft slipped out of her.

It would have been nice just to lie there next to each other for a while, content in the afterglow of their lovemaking.

That was exactly what they would have done, too, if the sound of hoofbeats nearby hadn't made Longarm sit up suddenly and reach for his Colt.

Chapter 13

Charlie scrambled up into a sitting position, too, and wrapped the blanket around her. Longarm came to his feet, Colt gripped in one hand while the other pulled his pants up. This interruption was damned bad timing. He wondered if the masked owlhoots were back.

That question was answered a moment later when a man's voice called, "Charlotte! Charlotte, if you can hear me, answer me!"

"That's Walt!" Charlie gasped. Without waiting for Longarm to say anything, she raised her voice and went on, "Walt! We're over here! Walt!"

The hoofbeats pounded closer. There were several horses approaching. Walt Conroy and some of his ranch hands, Longarm guessed.

Since it seemed unlikely there would be any shooting, he holstered his gun and bent down to stir the fire back into life. Blowing on the embers, he coaxed a small, flickering flame out of them and fed more branches to the fire until there was a sturdy little blaze going. As he straightened, four men on horseback rode up and reined in at the edge of the circle of light cast by the fire.

The one in the lead swung down quickly from his saddle. Ignoring Longarm, he went to Charlie and knelt beside her. "Are you all right, Charlotte?" he asked in clipped tones. He was tall and lean, with graying hair and a mustache. He looked plenty old enough to be Charlie's father, rather than her brother.

"I'm fine, Walt," she assured him. "And I've told you about calling me Charlie."

"Can't do it," he said stiffly. "Father named you Charlotte, and that's what I intend to call you."

Longarm thought that was a pretty silly argument to be having under the circumstances, what with Charlie sitting there with a bandaged-up leg, in the company of a strange man. So far Conroy hadn't paid much attention to those things, though.

That changed in the next moment as the cattleman looked down at Charlie's leg, which stuck part of the way out of the blanket. "What happened to you?" he asked. "You're hurt."

"A bullet scratched my leg," she told him.

Conroy finally turned his head to look at Longarm, a glare on his lean face. "Did you do this, mister?"

"No, Walt!" Charlie exclaimed, saving Longarm the trouble of a denial. "Custis patched up the wound. If he hadn't come along when I did, I'd probably be dead by now."

"Then who *did* shoot you?"

"Rustlers. I came across a bunch of them hazing some of our cattle off to God knows where."

Conroy sighed. "Let me guess what happened next. Instead of following them or coming to tell me about it, you opened fire on them."

"Seemed like the thing to do at the time," Charlie said, somewhat abashed.

"So one of those rustlers wounded you. How did you get away?"

"I didn't. They killed my horse and pinned me down in

these rocks. I was already wounded, and it was just a matter of time until they got me. Then Custis came along and ran them off."

Conroy straightened and turned to Longarm. "It sounds as though I owe you a debt of gratitude, mister . . . ?"

"Parker," Longarm supplied his alias. "Custis Parker." He took the hand that Conroy held out to him.

"How did you get rid of those men who were after my sister?" the rancher asked.

"Knocked out a couple of them, shot another and then made the rest think you and a bunch of your cowboys were riding up. I tricked 'em by wearing one of their own dusters and hoods."

"They were masked?" Conroy sounded surprised.

Longarm nodded. "Yeah. Couldn't see nothing of their faces except their eyes."

One of the cowboys who had ridden up with Conroy said, "Sounds like the same bunch that's been hittin' them gold shipments from the Oro Grande, boss."

"Impossible," Conroy snapped. "I'm convinced those miners are the ones responsible for the cattle we've lost."

Charlie had said the same thing earlier, but the idea still didn't sound convincing to Longarm. He asked, "Have you or your men ever seen any of the varmints who've been stealing your stock?"

"Not until today," Conroy answered grudgingly. "All the raids have taken place at night. The only ones who might have seen the rustlers were a couple of my nighthawks, and they were gunned down in cold blood. If the rustlers are going after Triangle C cows in broad daylight now, they're getting bolder, more reckless."

"Less afraid of getting caught," Longarm mused.

Charlie said, "Well, I didn't imagine the whole damned thing! This bullet graze on my leg ought to be proof enough of that."

Conroy turned back to her. "Of course you didn't imag-

113

ine it. No one is accusing you of that. The only thing you did wrong was to take matters into your own hands."

Charlie crossed her arms over her breasts and glared. "Somebody's got to," she said. "If those bastards ain't stopped, they'll strip this range clean!"

"The situation is a far cry from being that bad . . . yet." Conroy knelt beside her again. "How badly are you hurt?"

"I told you, just a graze. It bled a mite—"

"It bled quite a bit," Longarm corrected. "But I cleaned up the wound and bandaged it. I reckon it ought to heal all right."

"Sort of a delicate area for a man to be poking around at, especially when he doesn't even know the lady," Conroy said.

Coolly, Longarm replied, "I figured it was better to be a mite indelicate than to stand by and let the lady bleed to death, or let that wound start to fester."

"Yes, of course, you're right." Conroy stood again and looked down at Charlie. "Can you ride, or should I send the boys back to the ranch for the wagon?"

"I can ride," she said stubbornly. She started to push herself up. "Just let me get my feet under me . . ."

She went pale and sank back against the rock.

"Charlotte?" Conroy asked anxiously.

"Be better if somebody fetched that wagon," Longarm suggested. "Every time she starts to stand up, her head goes to spinning. I figure it's because of the blood she lost."

"Yes, I imagine so," Conroy agreed. "Charlotte, you stay right there. Don't move." He turned to his men. "Hank, you and Baldy ride back to headquarters as quickly as you can and fetch the wagon. Pile some blankets in the back of it so that it will be more comfortable. And send a rider to Medallion to bring Doctor Novak."

"I don't need a damn sawbones!" Charlie protested. "Custis fixed me up just fine."

"Yes, well, I'd rather have a professional opinion on that."

While Charlie was still muttering protests, the cowboys rode off, leaving Longarm there with Conroy and the third Triangle C hand. The cattleman said to Longarm, "You're welcome to spend the night at my ranch, Parker. It's the least I can do, considering all you've done for my sister."

Charlie snorted, and Longarm hoped she had the good sense not to say anything about *everything* he had done for her.

In hopes of precluding that, he said, "I'm much obliged. I was on my way out to the Triangle C anyway, to see if maybe you were hiring."

"You have experience as a cowboy?"

"I can make a hand," Longarm assured him. "I rode for a few spreads down in Texas."

That was true enough, although Longarm didn't explain that his experiences as a ranch hand were a decade and a half in the past. He had drifted west after the end of the war, the great clash between north and south that some referred to as the Late Unpleasantness. It was then that he had gone to cowboying and enjoyed the life, hard though it was, for a while before pinning on a badge and taking up law work. His skills were still good enough that he could pass for a regular puncher, if not a top hand.

Of course, he wasn't really looking for a job. He already had one, he reminded himself. He was a troubleshooter for Victor Jessup, owner of the Oro Grande mine and the sworn enemy of Walt Conroy.

Longarm smiled to himself. He seemed to have a knack for getting himself into these complicated, potentially dangerous situations.

"We'll talk about that job," Conroy said. "For now, though, just consider yourself my guest."

Longarm nodded. "Sounds good to me."

"You said something about shooting one of those rustlers. Did you kill him?"

"Yeah. His carcass is still over there in the trees, I reckon. I don't think his pards took the time to recover his body when they hightailed out of here, and they ain't been back since."

Conroy turned to the remaining cowboy. "Larribee, take a torch and ride over there. See if you can find that man."

"Sure, boss." The cowboy dismounted long enough to take a burning brand from the fire, then he swung back up and rode across the open ground toward the trees.

He was back a few minutes later with the corpse draped in front of his saddle. The horse high-stepped nervously, spooked by the dead man on his back. When the cowboy reached the fire, Conroy took hold of the dead man and hauled him off, letting him fall faceup on the ground. Charlie drew back a little from the corpse. She was tough, but it still had to be a little unnerving for her to see a dead man at such close range.

Conroy studied the rustler's face in the light of the fire. After a minute, he shook his head and said, "I don't think I've ever seen him before." He looked over at Longarm. "What about you, Parker?"

"I'm new in these parts," Longarm reminded him. "But I don't reckon I ever crossed trails with this hombre anywhere else, either."

"How about you, Larribee?"

"Never saw him before, boss," the cowboy replied.

Longarm hadn't taken the time to really look at the man when they traded shots in the trees. Now he saw that the rustler was cut from the same cloth as the one he'd knocked out. Hard, unshaven, angular features, worn range clothes, down-at-the-heel boots. The sort of drifting hard case who could be counted on to wide-loop some cows or hold up a stagecoach or steal an ore shipment.

The suspicion was growing in Longarm that the same gang was responsible for all those crimes. But men such as this hadn't planned those jobs. That had required someone

116

to bring them together, to make use of them. A ringleader of sorts . . .

"I suppose we ought to take his body to Medallion and turn him over to Sheriff Thacker," Conroy said. "I doubt that it'll do any good, though."

"The sheriff don't care about catching rustlers?" Longarm asked.

"Thacker is honest enough, I suppose. But he doesn't like to ruffle any feathers, especially those belonging to a man as wealthy and powerful as Victor Jessup. I wouldn't go so far as to say that the sheriff is in Jessup's pocket, but I don't expect a diligent investigation, either."

Longarm hoped Conroy was wrong about that, but he wouldn't be surprised if the rancher was right. Most local lawmen in the West were honest, hardworking star-packers, but some of them tended to walk soft around the most important folks in their communities.

About an hour later, the two cowboys Conroy had sent to fetch the wagon drove up in the vehicle, which was an old spring wagon with an uncovered bed piled high with blankets and quilts. Carefully, Longarm and Conroy helped Charlie to her feet and then lifted her into the back of the wagon. Conroy used some of the blankets to cover her.

The dead rustler was put back on Larribee's horse, despite the cowboy's good-natured grousing about having to carry a corpse around. Longarm put out the fire, and then the party started toward the Triangle C headquarters.

Longarm and Conroy rode alongside the wagon. From her nest in the back of it, Charlie asked, "How come you were out looking for me, Walt?"

"Why do you think we were looking for you? You rode to Medallion this morning, and you never came back."

"I was on my way home when I spotted those rustlers," she explained. "You shouldn't be worrying about me, though. I can take care of myself."

"Yes," Conroy said dryly. "So I see."

Even though it was too dark to tell, Longarm imagined Charlie was blushing in embarrassment and anger at her brother's words. "It was just bad luck that I got in a jam," she said defensively.

"Bad luck and poor judgment, you mean."

"It's just that I got all of Pa's gumption, I reckon."

"And his wife's recklessness."

"Don't go talking about my mama," Charlie warned.

"I'm not saying anything bad about her," Conroy replied. "She made Pa happy in his later years, and I'm grateful to her for that. But the doctor advised her that it might be dangerous for her to have children. No one really believed that Pa was still . . . I mean . . ."

"I know what you mean," Charlie said. "Nobody thought the old man could still sire a whelp, especially one like me."

Conroy sighed. "To be blunt about it, yes. But your mother went ahead and bore you anyway." His voice softened a little. "And although I'm sorry she didn't survive the birthing, I'm glad she was able to bring you into the world, Charlotte."

"Well, I'll be damned," Charlie said. "That may just be the nicest thing you've ever said to me . . . Walter."

Chapter 14

Conroy and his cowboys knew every foot of Triangle C range, so they had no trouble getting back to the ranch headquarters, even in the dark. Longarm studied it in the wash of silvery moonlight as they approached.

The ranch house was a sprawling log structure in the middle of a broad, shallow valley that was well-watered by a pair of creeks about half a mile apart. The house sat between the two streams. It was surrounded by pine and aspen. There was also a pair of large barns, extensive corrals, a blacksmith shop, a smokehouse, and a long bunkhouse for the hands. Even though he couldn't make out all the details in the dark, Longarm thought it was as nice a layout as he had seen in a while, and he said as much to Conroy.

He heard pride in the cattleman's voice as Conroy said, "You wouldn't think it started as a little greasy-sack outfit with less than fifty cows, would you?"

"Reckon it took a lot of years and a lot of hard work to build it up into the spread it is now."

"That's right. That's why I won't allow anything to threaten it. Or anybody, whether they be rustlers or high-handed mine owners."

Trying not to sound too much like a lawman asking

questions, Longarm said, "Why is it you think this Jessup fella wants to cause trouble for you?"

"His men have started fights with mine time and again, whenever my hands go into Medallion to pick up supplies or simply to blow off steam."

"Cowboys have been known to get into ruckuses before," Longarm pointed out.

"Yes, but Jessup has made it very plain that he considers ranching to be inferior to mining. He's arrogant."

Arrogance wasn't enough evidence to convict a fella of anything, thought Longarm, but he didn't say it.

"Not only that," Conroy went on, "but his mining operation threatens our water supply here on the Triangle C."

Longarm's interest perked up at that comment. Of such things sometimes real motives were made. He asked, "How's that?"

"Dogleg Creek runs down out of the mountains, but it doesn't flow nearly as much as it used to because tailings from the Oro Grande have clogged it. I complained to Jessup and he said that it was too bad. He even went so far as to say that he was thinking about damming it entirely because he might need the water to operate some hydraulic mining equipment."

"He hasn't done that, though?"

"Not yet," Conroy said grimly. "If he does . . . well, I don't like to think about what might happen if he does."

Longarm knew, though. Such a thing could easily lead to a shooting war, especially when Conroy and Jessup already disliked each other.

"That creek's not your only water source," he said. "You've got that other creek."

"It's smaller. There's not enough water in it to take care of all my stock. If we lose Dogleg . . . the Triangle C may not be able to make it."

Conroy wasn't thinking about it, of course, but he had just given Longarm a good reason to suspect that he was involved with the ore shipment robberies. If Conroy truly perceived the Oro Grande as a serious threat to the continued existence of the ranch, then he might try to protect the Triangle C by forcing Jessup out of business first.

Longarm considered himself a pretty good judge of character, though, and he just couldn't see a stiff-necked sort of man like Walt Conroy resorting to such underhanded tactics. Besides, there was evidence to indicate that the same bunch was behind both the rustling and the gold shipment holdups, which would rule out involvement by either side.

But as Charlie had said, anybody could put on a duster and a mask. Maybe there *were* two different bunches of troublemakers at work here, as unlikely as that seemed.

The wagon and its accompanying riders reached the ranch house a few minutes later. Longarm and Conroy helped Charlie into the house, where they were met by a large, white-haired woman.

"All right, you men," she said in a loud, booming voice, "give that poor girl to me. I'll get her upstairs to her own bed and see that she's taken care of. The doctor should be here soon."

"You sure you can handle her by yourself?" Longarm asked.

The woman gave him a withering look that told volumes about what a stupid question she considered that to be. She put an arm around Charlie's waist and easily helped her up the stairs to the second floor.

For the first time since Longarm had met him, Walt Conroy smiled. "Mrs. Keegan is quite capable. She's been the cook and housekeeper here for years, and I have no doubt she could bulldog a runaway steer if she needed to in order to protect Charlotte or myself."

"From what I've seen, I reckon you're probably right," Longarm agreed with a smile.

"I'm a little surprised she was able to restrain herself

from coming back out with the wagon, once Hank and Baldy told her Charlotte had been hurt. She probably thought she could do more good here, getting Charlotte's room ready and preparing something to eat."

"I thought I smelled something mighty good cooking," Longarm said.

"We'll likely have to wait until Charlotte has been fed and pampered for a while before Mrs. Keegan gets around to us. In the meantime, would you care for a drink?"

"Best offer I've had all day," Longarm said. That was an exaggeration, but only a slight one.

There was one big main room on the first floor of the ranch house that served as living room, study, office and dining room. Bearskin rugs lay on the floor, and one wall was taken up by a large fireplace, around which were arranged several pieces of heavy furniture. Conroy took a bottle and some tumblers from a glass-fronted sideboard.

"Tom Moore all right with you, Parker?" he asked as he held up the bottle.

Longarm had to grin at the sight of his favorite brand of Maryland rye. "You're a man after my own heart, Mr. Conroy," he said. "That'll do just fine."

Conroy poured the drinks. Longarm sipped the smooth liquor and felt its welcome warmth spreading through him. Warmth also came from the fireplace, where the fire had burned down but hadn't gone out. It would glow and flicker long into the night, at the rate it was going.

"There's a spare bedroom upstairs," Conroy said. "You're welcome to stay there tonight, rather than in the bunkhouse."

"I'm obliged, and I'll take you up on that offer. Been a while since I've slept in a real bed."

He had a hotel room with a bed in it back in Medallion, Longarm reminded himself, but fate had given him this chance to spend a little time on the Triangle C and find out more about the situation around here. He wasn't going to waste the opportunity.

Mrs. Keegan came downstairs while they were sipping their drinks, but she ignored them and didn't even glance in their direction as she bustled into the kitchen. She reappeared a minute later carrying a tray laden with plates of food that she took upstairs.

"What did I tell you?" Conroy asked with a faint smile. "Mrs. Keegan has been trying to make a proper young lady out of Charlotte for years without much success. Now that Charlotte is laid up for a while, I'm sure Mrs. Keegan will seize the opportunity to instruct her and lecture her on all the rules of behavior."

"I don't know your sister all that well," Longarm said, "but I've got a feeling she might buck a little at that."

"Yes, there's likely to be some head-butting going on. I intend to steer clear of it as much as possible."

That sounded like a good idea to Longarm.

Eventually, Mrs. Keegan came downstairs and called them into the dining room. Longarm hadn't eaten much all day, so he had a good appetite as he dug into a plate of roast beef and potatoes. There were biscuits and gravy, too, and apple pie for dessert.

The doctor came in while they were eating, having arrived from Medallion in his buggy. He was a small, wiry man with a tuft of gray beard, and he greeted Walt Conroy in a brisk but friendly fashion before going up to check on Charlie.

Longarm was full and content when he and Conroy finally pushed back from the table. The sawbones came downstairs a moment later, and Conroy asked him, "How is she, Doctor?"

"Miss Charlotte should be fine," Novak said. "I replaced the bandages with a fresh dressing. Her leg will be stiff and sore for a couple of weeks, and she'll have to be careful not to break the wound open, but whoever cleaned and bandaged it did a good job."

Conroy nodded toward Longarm and said, "That would be Parker here."

Dr. Novak regarded him speculatively. "Do you have medical training, young man?"

"Nope," Longarm said with a shake of his head. "Just more experience than I like to think about in patching up bullet holes."

Novak put on his hat. "Well, it was good work." To Conroy, he went on, "I'll be back in a day or two to look in on your sister, but I really think she'll be fine."

"Thank you, Doctor," Conroy said as he shook hands with the medico. Novak nodded to Longarm and went out.

"It's rather late," Conroy said to the big lawman. "I'm going to turn in shortly, but I'll show you to your room first. How about one more drink before we go upstairs?"

Longarm said, "Sounds fine to me," as he took out a cheroot and offered it to Conroy, who shook his head and filled a pipe instead. They had another drink and smoked for a few minutes in companionable silence.

"In the morning we'll talk about that job," Conroy promised as he showed Longarm to the spare bedroom.

"Sounds fine," Longarm said with a nod. He went inside, lit the lamp on the table beside the bed and then shut the door.

While he finished his cheroot, he took off his gunbelt and boots. Then he stripped down to the bottom half of his long underwear and stretched out on the bed, on top of the covers. The air in the room was a little chilly, but it felt good on his bare skin. He leaned over and blew out the lamp, then stared up at the ceiling in the darkness.

He didn't know if he was any closer to the objective that had brought him here or not. Conroy had to be considered a suspect in the gold shipment robberies, but Longarm didn't really believe the rancher had anything to do with them. His instincts told him that something else was going on here, that the situation in Medallion and the surrounding area was even more complex than it appeared to be on the surface. Longarm knew from experience that the best way to investigate such a case was to keep poking at it, like prodding a beehive until all the bees came swarming out.

Of course, when a fella did that, he risked being stung, too. . . .

He was thinking about bees and masked owlhoots when he finally dozed off.

Sunlight was slanting in past the curtains over the window when a voice whispered in his ear, "Custis, wake up."

He opened his eyes and turned his head and saw Charlotte Conroy's pretty face at close range. All the grime from the day before had been scrubbed off, and her hair smelled fresh and clean as it hung in shining blond wings around her face.

As pleasant as it was to wake up to such a vision, Longarm frowned and drew back a little. "Charlie?" he said quietly. "What are you doing here?"

He saw that she wore a silk robe that was belted tightly around her waist. When she leaned toward him, the top of it gapped open enough so that he could see down into the dark, enticing valley between her breasts. The firm globes were visible almost to the nipples.

"I feel a lot better this morning," she said with a suggestive smile.

"Well, I won't be feeling very good if your brother comes in and catches us like this. He'll probably go fetch a shotgun and a preacher."

"Pshaw. I don't want to get married. I just want to fool around with you. I never felt anything as good as having that big ol' thing of yours inside me."

"Yeah, it was mighty nice," he agreed, "but this ain't the

125

time or place for a repeat performance. Now skedaddle before somebody catches you in here."

Her hand delved under the covers and found his shaft, which had, with a mind of its own, grown hard due to Charlie's proximity. Lovingly, she stroked the erection through his long underwear.

"We could just do it for a little while . . ."

Heavy footsteps sounded in the hallway outside.

Charlie's head lifted, and she said, "Damn it! That sounds like Mrs. Keegan!"

A moment later they heard a knock on another door. Though muffled somewhat by the walls, Mrs. Keegan's voice was loud enough so that they had no trouble hearing her greeting. "Top of the mornin' to you, Miss Charlotte. How in the world are ye feelin' today—"

The way Mrs. Keegan paused abruptly made Charlie whisper, "Now the fat's in the fire."

The footsteps went back past Longarm's room and dwindled down the stairs. Charlie stood up and said, "She's gone to get Walt. This is my chance to get back to my room. I'll just tell them I was in the water closet. We have one, you know, with one of those new-fangled flush gadgets and everything."

"No, I didn't know," Longarm said. "You'd better hurry."

Charlie leaned down and pressed her mouth hard to his. "Another time," she said in a husky voice.

Then she was gone, leaving the room swiftly and limping only a little on her wounded leg.

Longarm lay back and put his hands under his head, sighing as he thought about the close call they'd just had. Charlie was a strong-willed, impulsive gal. He'd have to watch himself around her if he didn't want trouble to develop.

A few minutes later he heard Mrs. Keegan go past the room again, accompanied this time by Walt Conroy. Voices came to him, but he couldn't make out the words. He just knew that a discussion was going on between Charlie, her brother and the housekeeper.

Longarm swung his legs out of bed, stood up and began to pull his clothes on. It would be better if he were dressed by the time Conroy knocked on his door, as was bound to happen.

Sure enough, a few minutes later a sharp rapping sounded on the door. Longarm was wearing everything but his denim jacket and his Stetson as he opened it. Conroy stood there, a frown on his lean face.

"Good morning, Parker," the rancher greeted him. "Have you seen Charlotte this morning?"

No beating around the bush there. Longarm didn't particularly like lying, but he shook his head and said, "Nope. How's that bullet graze of hers doing?"

"Healing spectacularly already," Conroy replied. He appeared to accept Longarm's denial of seeing Charlie. "Charlotte has always had a very healthy constitution."

Longarm couldn't argue with that. He didn't comment on it at all, in fact.

"Come on down to breakfast whenever you're ready," Conroy went on.

"Thanks. I'll be there in a minute."

Conroy nodded and walked toward the stairs. Longarm left the door open as he shrugged into his jacket and settled his hat on his head. After a pause to check the sweep of his mustaches in the mirror on the wall, he left the room.

Charlie didn't come down for breakfast. Mrs. Keegan insisted on taking the meal up to her. The brief controversy seemed to be over. Charlie's story about being in the water closet when Mrs. Keegan looked in her room was reasonable enough, and it certainly couldn't be disproved. Longarm was just as glad she didn't join them for breakfast, though. That might have caused some tension at the table.

"Still want that riding job?" Conroy asked over flapjacks, bacon and steaming cups of Arbuckle's.

"Only if it's a real job," Longarm said. "I don't want you feeling beholden to me just because I gave your sister a hand."

"You saved her life, more than likely." Conroy took a sip of his coffee. "But that's not why I want to hire you. I have plenty of cow punchers."

"Well, then, in that case—"

Conroy held up a hand. "Let me finish. You can handle a gun, and the way you think fast in the middle of a crisis tells me that you're intelligent. You're just the sort of man I need, in fact."

"Need to do what?" Longarm asked warily.

"To track down those rustlers. Find out where their hideout is, so that the boys and I can raid it and put a stop to their depredations. The law can't or won't do it, so I have to take care of this problem myself. I think you're just the man to help me do it."

"So you want to hire me as a range detective?"

"That's right. You'll be free to come and go as you please, and you'll answer only to me."

Longarm tried not to grin. Victor Jessup had hired him to do pretty much the same job: find out who was responsible for the trouble and put a stop to it. And that was his assignment from Billy Vail, too. Conroy had played into Longarm's hand, just as Jessup had.

"It's a deal," he said.

"Excellent! As soon as we've finished breakfast, I'll take you out and show you the Triangle C."

"I'm looking forward to it," Longarm said honestly.

Chapter 15

During that morning, Longarm got a good look at the Triangle C, including Dogleg Creek. He could tell from studying the banks and the creek bed that the stream was lower now than it had been in the past.

Conroy hadn't exaggerated about how the Oro Grande mining operation had affected the creek. Most places in the West; water was an almost sacred thing. Men had fought and bled and died over water many times, in many places. Longarm had no doubt that they would again.

But it wouldn't happen here, not if he had anything to say about it.

"Tell me about the rustling," he said to Conroy as they reined in their horses on a rise overlooking the ranch headquarters. "How many head have you lost in all?"

"We'd have to do a gather to know for sure. At this time of year the herds are pretty spread out, you know."

Longarm nodded in understanding.

"But I'd estimate that we've lost at least five hundred head," Conroy continued. "The losses were small at first, twenty or thirty cows at a time. But the bastards have grown more daring. A couple of weeks ago they got over a hundred head in one raid. That's when I had two men killed."

Longarm heard the pain in the rancher's voice. Cowboys "rode for the brand," giving their utmost loyalty to the spread they worked for. Most cattlemen returned that loyalty to their punchers. Walt Conroy was obviously one such man.

"All these losses have been reported to the sheriff, I reckon?"

"Yes, but as I told you last night, I don't expect much from Sheriff Thacker. He's brought a posse out here a time or two and tried to follow the tracks the rustlers left, but he always lost the trail. The rustlers are good at covering up."

"Hard to move that many cows without leaving some tracks," Longarm commented.

"True, but there are several places where the ground becomes so rocky that cattle don't leave hoofprints. The rustlers drive the cows through one of those areas, and the trail is gone."

The trail wasn't *gone,* thought Longarm, it was just too faint for the sheriff to be able to follow it. A professional tracker might be a different story. Somebody like Al Sieber, who had scouted for General Crook during the Apache campaigns a few years earlier, could follow just about any trail, no matter how obscure. Longarm wasn't quite in Sieber's class as a tracker, but he was willing to bet that he was better at it than Sheriff Thacker.

He reminded himself that he really wasn't here to solve Conroy's rustling problems. He was after whoever had stolen those shipments of Oro Grande gold. But he still couldn't shake the feeling that the crimes were connected.

"I'll see how far I can track the cows they got off with yesterday," he told Conroy, "and then I'll probably ride back into Medallion."

Conroy frowned. "Why go back to Medallion? The rustling is going on out here."

"Those rustlers don't live on the Triangle C, though," Longarm pointed out. "They've got to go somewhere after they get through stealing your cows. They probably have the stolen stock penned up somewhere, and some of the gang will be on guard there all the time, but the others ride into town, I'll bet. Thought I'd ask around, see if anybody's suddenly got more money than they ought to have."

Conroy shrugged and said, "Do whatever you think is best. If I was a detective I would have tracked them down myself before now, I suppose."

"Don't worry," Longarm said. "I'll stay in touch."

He turned his buckskin to ride away, but Conroy stopped him by saying, "Wait a minute. We haven't talked about your wages yet."

"Wait until I've got some results to show you," Longarm told him. "Then we can talk about what it's worth."

Of course, he had no more intention of drawing wages from Conroy than he did of taking Jessup's money. He didn't figure he was actually playing both sides against the middle as long as he wasn't being paid by the bitter enemies.

He had a knack for finding his way around, especially in places where he had been before, so he didn't have any trouble finding the spot where Charlie had been pinned down by the rustlers the day before. From there he was able to backtrack the men who had pursued Charlie with guns blazing.

The tracks he found confirmed her story. The rustlers had been pushing a jag of about fifty cattle toward the eastern boundary of Triangle C range when some of them had suddenly veered off. Those were the men who had gone after Charlie. What looked like four or five other men had stayed with the cows and kept them moving.

Longarm didn't know where the boundary line was, but by the time he had followed the trail of the stolen cattle for several miles, he thought that he must be getting close to it. Then the tracks led him into a wasteland of red sandstone spires and narrow gullies and sun-blasted flats. The trail disappeared on the hard, rocky ground, and no matter how much he cast back and forth for it, he couldn't find it again.

Reining in, he cuffed his hat back and frowned at the ugly terrain in front of him. It might indeed take an Al Sieber or someone of his talent to follow this trail. Longarm could see why Sheriff Thacker had been forced to give up.

He thought about plunging into the wasteland and searching blindly for some sign of the stolen cows, but he knew he didn't have the time to do that. He had to get back to Medallion and continue that end of the investigation. Reluctantly, he turned the buckskin and rode west again.

It was past midday when he came to the stage road. He turned north and followed it to Medallion. When he reached the settlement he put up his horse at the stage line corral and then walked toward the Cattle King Saloon. He was hungry, and he recalled with fondness the saloon's free lunch.

Before he could get there, he ran into Claude Brandstett, the newspaper editor. The journalist stopped him and said, "Mr. Parker, isn't it? You work for Mr. Jessup now?"

"That's right," Longarm said.

"Do you know when Mr. and Mrs. Jessup will return from the Oro Grande?"

"Supposed to be back today, I think. That party they're giving is tomorrow night."

"So it is," Brandstett said. "You'll be attending?"

"I'll be there," Longarm said without going into the details of why he would be in attendance.

"I'd like to interview you about that stage holdup you prevented. From what I've heard it must have been quite an adventure."

About the last thing Longarm wanted to do was to sit down and answer a bunch of questions from this fella. He said, "Sure, maybe we can do that sometime. Right now I'm a mite busy. . . ."

"Of course." Brandstett lifted his bowler hat. "Good day, Mr. Parker."

Longarm went on to the Cattle King. Salty was off on his stagecoach run, and Longarm sort of missed the old jehu. Salty was a surprisingly observant cuss. Longarm would have liked to ask him about what had gone on in Medallion while he was out at the Triangle C.

He got a beer from the bartender, filled a plate at the free lunch counter and went over to sit down at a table near the stage. As he sat there eating and sipping from his mug of beer, piano music began to come from behind the curtain that closed off his view of most of the stage.

Curious, he looked through the small gap in the curtain, and his interest grew stronger as he saw a girl walk past up there, holding some papers in her hand. She stopped where Longarm could see her.

She was small, but the curves of her body in the gray dress she wore told him that she was a grown woman. Thick, glossy black hair fell around her shoulders. When she turned a little, Longarm could see that the papers she held were sheet music. She was listening to the piano player and following the notes on the pages. Suddenly, she sang a few words, her voice quiet but clear and well-pitched.

For a second, Longarm was reminded of Glorieta McCall, the singer who had been known as the Arizona Flame because of her beautiful red hair. She had been involved in the same case as Salty.

Longarm put those memories out of his head to concentrate on the here and now. The girl on the stage moved out of his view and then a moment later strolled back into sight again, still studying the sheet music in her hand. This time she was turned toward Longarm, however, and she must have sensed his eyes on her because she looked up, met his gaze and smiled.

Longarm lifted his beer mug in a salute and gave the girl a friendly smile in return. She turned away and returned to her practicing, but not before giving him one last coquettish glance over her shoulder.

There were other saloons in Medallion besides the Cattle King. Longarm drifted from place to place during the afternoon, nursing drinks, talking to bartenders, playing a hand of cards here and there. His years of experience had taught him how to ask questions without appearing to do so. By evening he knew plenty of gossip about what was going on in town.

He heard that Regina Jessup had a reputation for being unfaithful to her husband. She could play lady of the manor all she wanted to, but she had some pretty coarse appetites, according to the whispers and snickers Longarm heard. Of course, after what had happened at the Cottonwood stage station, nobody was telling him anything about Regina that he didn't already know.

If Regina's affairs were such common knowledge, how come Jessup didn't know about them? Or maybe he did, and for some unknown reason chose to ignore them. Was there any way to tie that in with the gold robberies? If so, Longarm didn't see it.

He ate supper in a little hash house—also a good place to pick up gossip, although he didn't hear any that was particularly interesting while he was there—and then drifted back toward the Cattle King. As he approached the saloon, he noticed Deputy Dave Bardwell lounging along the boardwalk on the other side of the street.

Longarm frowned. Now that he thought about it, he had seen Bardwell quite a bit during the afternoon. It was almost like the deputy had been following him. Every time Longarm had come out of a saloon or dance hall or gambling den, Bardwell had been somewhere close by.

Longarm knew Bardwell didn't like him. Obviously, the deputy was suspicious of him as well.

Pretending to ignore Bardwell, Longarm went into the Cattle King. Now there was a sign on a stand near the stage, announcing that Miss Constance Maxwell would be performing a medley of songs from the productions of Gilbert and Sullivan. Longarm knew without having to think about it that Constance Maxwell was the pretty girl he had seen on stage earlier in the day, the one who had smiled at him.

Even though the day hadn't been very productive, he supposed he could take the time to see a show, especially one put on by a girl as beautiful as Constance Maxwell. He got a beer at the bar and found an empty chair at a table occupied by a couple of cowboys who didn't mind if he joined them.

It wasn't long until the curtain was pulled back and the slick-haired musician seated at the piano on the stage began to play. Constance Maxwell strolled out onto the stage, wearing a fancy, low-cut gown. Her raven hair was put up in an elaborate arrangement of curls and had a bright red rose tucked into it. She was breathtakingly lovely.

When she began to sing, her voice was equally lovely. Longarm found himself paying rapt attention. So was every other man in the place. The normal hubbub of a frontier saloon died away as everyone turned toward the girl and listened to her sing.

Longarm wasn't so distracted that he failed to notice Dave Bardwell come into the saloon. The deputy stood at the far end of the bar, but his attention was turned on Constance just like that of everybody else in the room. Or was it? Longarm saw Bardwell looking at him, too.

The audience erupted in applause when Constance finished her performance. She sang one short encore and then left the stage to more applause. Clearly she was a favorite of the cowboys and miners who patronized the Cattle King.

She came out a short time later, dressed more demurely now, and mingled with the customers, bestowing smiles and laughs on them and making these hardened frontiersmen as bashful as blushing schoolboys. She played them expertly, pausing at a table or a spot along the bar for a few moments and then moving on before any of her multitude of admirers could grow jealous. Eventually she worked her way over to the table where Longarm sat.

"Hello, boys," she said to him and the two cowboys who also sat at the table. Looking at Longarm, she went on, "I remember you. You're the one who was watching me practice this afternoon."

Longarm took off his hat. "Yes, ma'am. I knew from what I heard then that I'd be in for a treat if I came back tonight. Your show was even better than I expected, though."

"My, aren't you the gallant one. What's your name?"

"Custis Parker, ma'am."

She gave him a cool, smooth hand. "I'm pleased to meet you, Custis."

Longarm supposed it was inevitable that things wouldn't continue to go smoothly. He was about to say something else when one of the miners came up behind Constance and put a hand on her shoulder.

"Hey, honey, come talk to some real men," the miner said in a loud, drunken voice. "You don't want to waste your time on these cowboys."

One of the punchers at the table stood up and glared at the miner. "Go back to your tunnel, rock-eater. You ain't wanted here."

The miner glowered back at him. "At least the shaft o' the Oro Grande don't stink of cowshit!" he said.

"No, it stinks of rock-eaters, and that's worse!"

The girl said quickly, "Boys, boys, there's no need to argue. I like all of you, and I'm glad you came to hear me sing tonight—"

"I'd like to do a whole lot more than listen to you sing, darlin'," the miner said with a leer. He still had hold of her shoulder, and he started to tug on it. "C'mon with me now. I'll show you a mighty fine time."

"You let go of the lady!" the other cowboy yelled as he sprang to his feet.

"Make me, you damn cow nurse!" the miner shot back.

That was all it took. A second later, as Constance yelped in alarm and ducked out of the way, the men began flailing away at each other. The loud, angry voices had drawn plenty of attention, and as fists began to fly, more men converged on the table. Some were cowboys and some were miners, and within mere moments the brawl began to spread across the room.

Longarm came to his feet, looped an arm around Constance Maxwell, and said, "I'll get you out of here, ma'am!" He shouldered his way through the milling crowd toward a nearby door, keeping his left arm around Constance and using his right to fend off the brawling combatants. After a few tense moments, they reached the door, and Longarm jerked it open.

As he hustled Constance through the door, they found themselves in a hallway. Longarm kicked the door shut behind them just as a thrown chair crashed into it.

"Damn it!" Constance burst out. "Why do so many of my performances have to end this way?"

"It doesn't have anything to do with you, ma'am," Longarm assured her. "Miners and cowboys just naturally don't get along too well."

"I don't care, I'm tired of it." She sighed and shook her head. "Thank you, Custis. If you hadn't gotten me out of there, there's no telling what might have happened to me."

"None of those hombres would have hurt you on purpose, ma'am," he told her.

"Call me Connie," she said. "And it wouldn't have mattered whether it was on purpose or not, I still could have been hurt."

"I reckon that's true."

"I'd like to do something to pay you back for your help." That coquettish smile appeared on her face again.

"Would you like to come up to my room and have a drink with me?"

Longarm was only human. There was no way he could refuse an invitation like that.

"Lead the way," he said with a smile.

Chapter 16

It was inevitable, of course. They'd had some brandy, and then Connie had curled up on Longarm's lap as he sat in a big armchair and she started kissing him. One thing led to another and clothes started to come off, and almost before he knew it, he found himself lying on his back in her bed, stark naked, while Connie, equally nude, poised herself over his groin and held his massively erect shaft in her soft fingers, aiming it at the heated opening between her legs.

"Are you sure this is going to fit inside me, Custis?" she asked. "It's awfully big."

"Only one way to find out," Longarm said.

"Well, yes, that's true." Connie lowered her hips, and the tip of his member touched wet, hot, female flesh. She slid down onto him, slowly impaling herself on the great goad of his manhood. When she reached bottom, she gasped and said, "Oh! Oh, yes, it fits . . ."

She rocked her hips back and forth, causing him to slide in and out of her a little. It was hard to believe that such a tiny girl could engulf him that way, but she managed without any trouble. He felt the surprising strength in her muscles as she rode him. Cupping her firm breasts, he used his thumbs to toy with the hard, pebbled nipples.

The passion that their coupling aroused in them was so strong that Longarm knew it couldn't be denied for long. Neither of them wanted to delay the climax that was poised to break over them like a huge wave. Longarm shifted his grip to her hips to steady her as he began to drive up into her at a hard and fast pace. Connie cried out as she began to spasm.

Longarm gave himself over to his own culmination, exploding inside her. He shuddered as he emptied himself into her. With a long sigh, she sagged forward, sprawling on his broad, muscular chest. He put one arm around her while he used the other hand to stroke her hair and her back and her still-quivering hips.

"That was so good, Custis," she whispered. "I knew as soon as I saw you this afternoon that I wanted to do this. I knew it would be wonderful."

"You're a mighty good fortune-teller, then," he said.

"No. A woman knows these things. Her instinct tells her when she's meant to be with a particular man."

They lay there snuggling together for several minutes before Connie reluctantly disengaged herself and got out of bed. She walked over to the sideboard.

"Another drink?" she asked Longarm.

"All right," he said. "Sounds good."

With her back to him, she poured the brandy and then brought the glass over to him as he sat up with his back propped against the bed's headboard. Adorably nude, she perched beside him and handed him the drink. She had one of her own that she sipped. Longarm lifted the glass to his lips, took a healthy swallow of the smooth liquor . . .

"Well, son of a bitch!" he exclaimed as he slapped the palm of his hand down on the rough-hewn table in Salty's cabin.

The old-timer jumped a little. "What in blazes took a bite outta you, Custis?"

Longarm had been completely lost in the memories of the past few days, examining each of them closely as they came back to him and filled in the gaps in what he had recalled. Now the present came flooding in, and with it the realization that while he had answered some of the questions that had plagued him, he had new ones to replace them.

"I know what happened, at least most of it," he said to Salty, "but I'm damned if I know *why*."

"You still reckon Dave Bárdwell's the one who tried to frame you for killin' Miz Jessup?"

"He had a hand in it, I expect," Longarm said grimly, "but he wasn't alone. He couldn't have slipped me that Mickey Finn. Somebody else did that."

Salty leaned forward. "Who?"

"I don't remember anything after Connie Maxwell gave me a drink of brandy in her room at the saloon last night . . . not until I woke up this morning with Regina Jessup's body in my bed."

Salty's rheumy eyes widened. "Connie? That sweet lil' gal who sings at the Cattle King? Damn, Custis, I'm havin' a hard time believin' that she'd be mixed up in somethin' as ringy as this."

"It's the only explanation that makes sense," Longarm said stubbornly. "Knockout drops take effect in a hurry. If somebody had slipped a dose in one of the drinks I had earlier in the evening, I wouldn't have stayed awake as long as I did. It had to be Connie."

"Say, what was you doin' in her room, anyway?" As soon as he had asked the question, Salty held up a hand to forestall Longarm's answer. "Never mind. I reckon I can guess close enough. Gals always did find you pert-near irresistible, Custis."

"Sometimes that's more of a curse than a blessing, old son," Longarm said in a solemn voice.

After a moment, Salty asked, "What're you gonna do now?"

Longarm tugged at his earlobe and then scraped his thumbnail along his jawline. "I ain't sure. If Connie was part of the frame-up, that means she's got to be connected to Regina's murder, too. At least she had to know about it."

"Mebbe not," Salty argued. "Maybe she just doped you figurin' on robbin' you. I've heard o' such things."

Longarm thought it over and nodded. "And Bardwell could have been in on it with her. There's no way Connie could have gotten me out of her room by herself while I was knocked out. She's just a little thing—"

"And you're a pretty big galoot," Salty finished.

"Yeah, I am," Longarm agreed with a weary smile. He grew more serious again as he went on, "So let's say Connie and Bardwell were in it together. Why me? I ain't a rich man."

"No, but as far as they know you're workin' for one."

"Jessup."

"Yep. They could've thought he'd given you some o' your wages in advance."

Longarm rubbed his chin in thought. "Still, it doesn't seem likely he would have advanced me enough to make me a good target for being drugged and robbed. Maybe they wanted something else . . ." He banged a fist on the table as a thought occurred to him.

"Keep that up and you're gonna bust the table," Salty said.

Longarm ignored the warning and went on, "When I woke up, my badge and identification papers were gone. Bardwell had been following me around all day. He was already suspicious of me. He wanted to find out if I was telling the truth about who I am. So he got Connie to drug me and knock me out, so that he could search my pockets."

Bardwell probably hadn't told Connie to take him to bed first, thought Longarm. He had a feeling that had been Connie's idea.

"So they found your bona fides and knew you was a

lawman," Salty said. "How do you get from that to wakin' up with a dead woman in your bed?"

"I don't know. Let me chew that last bite of apple a little longer."

Taking out a cheroot, Longarm snapped a lucifer to life on an iron-hard thumbnail and set fire to the gasper as he thought over the scenario that he and Salty were piecing together. He was fairly certain Bardwell had taken him through the rear hallways and alleys that he had traversed earlier in the day, moving him from Connie's room in the Cattle King to the room he had rented in the Horton House, all while he was out cold. Had Regina Jessup been killed after that, or was she already dead?

Something tugged at his thoughts. He remembered when he had been alone in Connie's room that morning, after fleeing the hotel and killing the bushwhacker in the alley. Connie had left, ostensibly to complain to Claude Brandstett about the newspaper story concerning her singing. Probably, though, she had gone to warn Dave Bardwell that their attempt to frame Longarm had failed . . . which Bardwell already knew because he had busted into the hotel room and seen that Longarm had gotten away.

That wasn't what was bothering Longarm. He recalled that someone else had slipped into Connie's room and called her name while he lurked behind the privacy screen. The voice has been distorted by the fact that its owner was whispering, but still, there had been something familiar about it . . . Longarm thought he ought to know who it belonged to.

He couldn't pin down the memory, though. With a shake of his head, he put it aside for the moment.

"Come up with anything?" Salty asked.

"Not really. I don't know who had a reason for killing Mrs. Jessup, and I don't know why whoever did it decided to stash the body in my room and place the blame on me."

"Well, you can't wander around town when you're

wanted for killin' the wife o' the richest man in these parts."

"That's just it," Longarm said. "Jessup introduced me to Sheriff Thacker, and Thacker didn't act like anything was wrong. There's no manhunt going on around the settlement, either."

Salty frowned. "You reckon Bardwell didn't say nothin' about Miz Jessup bein' dead?"

"He must not have, for reasons of his own."

"Then . . . Lord have mercy! . . . You reckon she's still there?"

"I think I'm going to have to find out," Longarm said.

Salty insisted on going with him. As they walked from the old-timer's cabin along Medallion's main street, Longarm saw that the settlement was still relatively quiet, with no more activity going on than there would be on a normal day. There was certainly no uproar as there would have been if a full-scale hunt for a murderer was going on.

"You gonna just walk right into the hotel bold as brass?" Salty asked.

"Don't see any reason not to," replied Longarm. "I've still got the room key." He had already slipped his hand in his pocket to make sure that was true.

The clerk appeared to pay no attention to them as they crossed the lobby to the stairs. They went up to the second floor and along the corridor to the door of Longarm's room.

Longarm had to admit that he felt a mite nervous as he put the key in the lock, turned it and opened the door. His right hand hovered near the butt of his Colt as he stepped into the room with Salty right behind him.

The room was empty.

Longarm took a deep breath when he saw that Regina Jessup's body was gone. For that matter, so were the bloody bedclothes and even the mattress. Longarm looked quickly around the room. There was no blood on the floor or anywhere else. Somebody had stripped the room completely of any traces of Regina's murder.

Salty eased the door closed and said, "Where in tarnation did she go? A corpse don't just get up and wander off all by its ownself!"

"No, somebody took her out of here and hid her somewhere else," Longarm said. "They took the bloody sheets and the mattress, too, so there wouldn't be any evidence."

"Dave Bardwell?"

"That's my guess, but we still don't know for sure."

Salty shook his head. "These waters are gettin' too damn deep and murky for me. Crooked lawmen, knockout drops, dead bodies that don't stay put . . . If you can make any sense outta this, Custis, you're a whole heap smarter'n me!"

"Don't forget gold shipment hijackings, wide-looped cows and stagecoach holdups," Longarm said with a humorless smile. "The varmints have been might busy around here of late."

"You reckon the same bunch is behind all of it?"

"That's what I'm thinking right now. The way this case has been going, something else will probably come along in a few minutes and knock that idea into a cocked hat, too."

They left the hotel, and Longarm led the way around back of the building, to the alley where he'd had the shootout with the waiting bushwhacker. Not surprisingly, that body was gone, too, and dirt had been kicked over the blood that had spilled in the alley when the gunman fell. If not for the dark stains he uncovered by scuffing around with his boots, a small part of Longarm's brain might have begun to wonder if he had imagined the whole crazy thing.

He knew it was true, though, and the blood proved it.

"Salty, you know most of the men around here, don't you?" Longarm asked.

"I reckon I do."

"You think you could find me eight good men who'd like to earn some of Mr. Jessup's money tonight?"

Salty scratched at the bristles of his beard. "Mebbe. What you want 'em to do?"

"I'm in charge of guarding that big party at the Jessup mansion. I need some armed men to station outside. I'd be obliged if you could come, too."

"I reckon I could do that. Stage don't head back to Kingman until tomorrow. But I don't understand . . . Miz Jessup's dead. How can she throw a party?"

"She can't, but I've got a feeling that soiree's gonna go on anyway."

"All right, I'll round up some fellas for you, and I'll be there, too. But danged if I can figure this out."

Longarm was beginning to get a glimmer or two, but there were still plenty of pieces of the puzzle to put together. "Thanks, Salty," he said. "I'll see you later. You and the other men meet me at the Jessup house around dark."

"Sure. Where will you be until then?"

"Stirring the pot," Longarm said.

Chapter 17

He walked around the block and up to the entrance of the
Cattle King. The horses that had been ridden in earlier by
Walt Conroy, his sister Charlie and several of the Triangle
C hands were still tied at the hitch rack.

Now that he remembered everything that had happened,
Longarm was surprised that Charlie Conroy had ridden
into town with her brother and the other men. That bullet
graze on her thigh was only about forty-eight hours old.
Her leg had to be pretty sore and she shouldn't have been
on it at all, let alone riding around on horseback.

But Charlie was plenty stubborn, Longarm reminded
himself, and she obviously had a way of wrapping her
much older brother around her little finger. If she had insisted on coming along, in the end Walt would have let her
have her own way.

Longarm hadn't noticed Charlie limping when she went
into the saloon earlier, but at the time he didn't remember
that she had been wounded by rustlers, so he hadn't been
looking for any sign of her injury. She had been surrounded by the Triangle C punchers, too, so he hadn't gotten that good a look at her.

He pushed the batwings aside and stepped into the saloon. The place was busy, though not as much so as it would be later in the afternoon or that night.

Walt Conroy and Charlie sat at a table near the stage, Longarm saw as he looked around the room. The cowboys who had come into town with them were lined up at the bar. Brice MacPhail stood there, too, drinking with his fellow punchers. Longarm hadn't seen MacPhail during his visit to the Triangle C, but there was nothing all that unusual about that. At any given time on a big ranch, some of the hands were out at isolated line shacks or combing the brush for strays. MacPhail had simply been occupied elsewhere while Longarm was on the Triangle C range.

Longarm walked over to the table where Conroy and Charlie sat. They both looked up and greeted him with smiles. Without waiting for an invitation, Longarm pulled back a chair and sat down.

"Didn't expect to see you in town today," he said to Charlie. "Shouldn't you be resting that wounded leg of yours?"

"I got bored," she said defensively. "Have you ever tried to just lay around and do nothing?"

"Only when I had to, and I can't say as I liked it," Longarm admitted. "Still, you'd better be careful. You don't want to hurt it worse."

Charlie snorted. "Walt tried the same argument. You see how far it got him."

Conroy said, "I've learned over the years, Parker, that a man can butt his head against a stone wall for only so long before knocking his brains out. I generally stop before I get to that point with Charlotte." The rancher leaned forward and lowered his voice. "Have you found out anything about the rustling?"

"I've got an idea or two," Longarm said truthfully, "but no proof of anything yet. I'm hoping it won't take much longer to come up with some, though. Anything else happen out on the ranch?"

Conroy shook his head. "It was a quiet night. Those wide-loopers haven't been back."

"That's good. Maybe they won't have a chance to raid the place again before we get them rounded up."

As Longarm finished speaking, he heard a footstep behind him and saw Charlie glance up. An angry voice asked, "What are you doin' with this fella?"

"I don't know that that's any of your business, Brice," Conroy snapped.

"But for your information," Charlie added, "this is Custis Parker."

"The one who saved you from those rustlers?" Brice MacPhail asked with the familiar sneer in his voice as he stepped alongside the table. "You might not have such a high opinion of him, Charlie, if I told you he was in Connie Maxwell's room this mornin', actin' mighty familiar with her."

Charlie caught her breath. "Is that true, Custis?" she asked. "Were you with that . . . that singer?" She might as well have said *whore* from the way she made it sound.

MacPhail didn't give Longarm a chance to answer. The big cowboy said, "He was in her room, all right, and she was just gettin' out of the bathtub when I caught 'em like that—"

Conroy cut in, "A fellow might wonder just what *you* were doing in a situation like that, Brice."

"I don't wonder at all," Charlie said. "He's in love with Connie Maxwell. He always has been, ever since the first time he saw her." Charlie switched her gaze back to Longarm. "But that doesn't explain what you were doing there, Custis."

Charlie had grown up wild, according to Salty, and she was about as rough and plainspoken as any cowboy. But she was still a woman, and obviously the time she had shared with Longarm had meant enough to her so that MacPhail's insinuations were causing her to be a mite jeal-

149

ous. With everything else he already had on his plate, Longarm didn't need this added complication, but he didn't see any way of avoiding it. Best just to tell the truth.

Some of it, anyway.

"I was there," he said, not mentioning anything about how he wound up in Connie's room by accident, after waking up with a dead woman in his bed and having a shootout with a bushwhacker.

"I see," Charlie replied coolly. "Well, some men prefer the company of cheap, no-account women—"

"Hold on!" MacPhail exclaimed. "You can't talk about Connie that way!"

"Be careful, Brice," Conroy warned. "You still ride for the Triangle C."

"Well, maybe it's time for me to draw my pay and ride on," MacPhail blustered.

"That's up to you."

"Maybe I will . . . but there's somethin' I got to do first."

With that he turned, pivoting smoothly at the hips, and swung a big fist that landed solidly on Longarm's jaw.

Longarm had seen the punch coming, but it was too fast for him to get out of the way. His chair went over backward as the blow exploded on his jaw. He sprawled on the sawdust-littered floor, sliding a few inches before he came to a stop.

The impact had started bells ringing in his brain. Over their racket, he vaguely heard yelling. He blinked his eyes and worked his jaw back and forth to make sure it wasn't broken. When he looked up, he saw Charlie Conroy on her feet, swinging punches at Brice. He had a hand on her shoulder, holding her back so that she couldn't reach him.

"You dirty coward!" she raged. "That was the most low-down thing I ever saw!"

Her brother grabbed hold of her and pulled her back, away from Brice MacPhail. "Blast it, Charlie, take it easy!" he said, forgetting in the heat of the moment to call her Charlotte. "You'll break that wound open and start it bleeding again!"

MacPhail stood there grinning, rubbing the knuckles of the hand he had used to clout Longarm.

"As for you, Brice," Conroy went on, "you won't have to quit. You're fired! Show your face on the Triangle C range again and I'll have you horsewhipped!"

"Fine," MacPhail grated. "It's worth it to see that bastard Parker wallowin' on the floor like . . . like . . ."

Longarm began climbing to his feet.

MacPhail's voice trailed off as a frown creased his forehead. When Longarm was upright, the big cowboy said, "Damn it, you ought to be out cold! When I hit a man like that, he goes down and stays down!"

"As you're about to find out, old son," Longarm rasped, "I ain't just any man."

He lunged at MacPhail, swinging his right fist in a roundhouse blow. MacPhail bit on the feint and moved to his right, directly into the path of the straight left that Longarm snapped out. Longarm's fist crashed into MacPhail's face and knocked him back a step.

Quick to try to follow up on the advantage, Longarm rushed in and hooked a right to MacPhail's belly. The big cowboy's breath, laden with whiskey fumes, gusted out into Longarm's face. Longarm threw a left cross that jerked MacPhail's head around. The next punch was a right that sent MacPhail flying backward onto a table. The table's legs snapped, and it crashed to the floor with MacPhail landing among the debris.

The room had gone quiet when MacPhail threw his treacherous punch, but it erupted in shouts as Longarm struck back with that flurry of blows. Silence again fell when MacPhail did. A couple of the Triangle C punchers lined up at the bar took a step forward, their faces angry at the sight of their comrade lying on the floor of the saloon.

Walt Conroy raised a hand to stop the men from advancing on Longarm. His voice rang across the big room as he said, "Brice had it coming, boys! He doesn't ride for Triangle C anymore!"

"In that case," one of the cowboys called to Longarm, "give the son of a bitch one for me if he gets up, mister!"

Longarm grinned as he wiped the back of a hand across his mouth. The cowboys had been willing to come to MacPhail's defense as long as they thought he still rode for the brand, but now that they knew otherwise, their sympathies switched sides. Clearly, MacPhail had been tolerated, but he was not well liked on the Triangle C.

The question now was whether or not MacPhail was going to get up. He was groggy but not out cold. He rolled onto his side, pushed himself up on an elbow and shook his head, trying to clear some of the cobwebs from it. Blood dripped from his nose and mouth. He turned his head, looked up at Longarm and grated, "I'm gonna kill you, you bastard."

"You're welcome to try," Longarm said. His heart pounded in his chest and blood raced through his veins. The last of the hangover he had felt from being drugged was gone now, and after several days of trying to untangle the labyrinth of motives and suspects around Medallion, it felt surprisingly good to face a direct threat head-on. He laughed in anticipation as Brice MacPhail shoved up from the littered wreckage of the broken table and came at him again.

Everyone had drawn back to give them room. Conroy and Charlie stood by the table where they had been sitting, anxious looks on their faces as they watched. Shouts went up from the other spectators as MacPhail charged in like a bull, swinging wild punches.

Longarm was able to block most of the blows, but one slipped through his guard and clipped him on the side of the head, staggering him. MacPhail might be a son of a bitch, but he was plenty strong. Longarm recovered and whipped a left-right combination to MacPhail's face that rocked the cowboy's head back and forth. More like a bull than ever, MacPhail lowered his head and drove his shoulder into Longarm's body, ramming the big lawman backward.

Both men crashed down on another table, breaking it to pieces. The damages were going to be high by the time they were through. MacPhail grabbed one of the broken table legs and swung it at Longarm's head, drawing angry shouts from the crowd. Longarm rolled aside just in time as the table leg slammed into the floor where his head had been a second earlier.

He snapped a kick to MacPhail's chest that knocked the cowboy backward and made him drop the makeshift club. Longarm dived after him and came down on top of him. He got his left hand on MacPhail's throat and pinned him down for a second while he drove a couple of rights into his face, pulping MacPhail's nose even worse than it already was. MacPhail heaved his body up desperately, throwing Longarm off.

Longarm fell to the side, rolled over and scrambled to his feet as MacPhail got up and came after him again. He met MacPhail's rush squarely. For a long moment, the two men stood toe to toe, slugging it out, seeing which of them could inflict the most damage while withstanding the damage that was being heaped on him. Longarm tasted blood in his mouth, and some swelling above his left eye distorted his vision a little. He could still see to hit MacPhail, though, and in this moment of sheer barbaric fervor, that was all that mattered.

MacPhail swung and missed, and Longarm stepped in with a haymaker right that wasn't a feint this time. He put all the strength and speed he had left into the blow, and it landed pure and hard on MacPhail's jaw with a sound like the blade of an ax sinking deep into a block of wood. MacPhail twisted halfway around and stood there for a heartbeat before dropping to his knees. He swayed back and forth once like a tree about to topple and then pitched forward onto his face, out cold.

Longarm had put so much into the punch that even though it landed on its target, he stumbled forward a couple of steps. He had to slap his hands down on a table to catch his balance. His head hung forward for a minute. As he looked down at his hands, he saw a crimson drop of blood from his mouth land on the back of his right hand and splatter across the tanned skin. There was a roaring in his head, but after a moment he became aware of someone calling his name. It sounded like Charlie Conroy. She said something else, but what was it?

Look out. That was it. Charlie had yelled, "Custis, look out!"

He straightened and started to turn toward Charlie and her brother, but another figure loomed up and blocked his view of them. He saw the angry face of Sheriff Rip Thacker and saw as well the butt of the shotgun coming at him. Longarm didn't have enough left to get out of the way.

The lights went out, and so did Longarm.

Chapter 18

Waking up was always better than the alternative, but it was still a mighty painful experience, Longarm found as he crawled up out of the darkness of oblivion into the light of awareness. It hurt like hell, in fact.

He had taken such a pounding from Brice MacPhail's fists that every muscle in his body ached. His head throbbed, his bruised lips stung and his left eye didn't want to open. It seemed to be glued shut with something, probably dried blood. He opened his right eye in a narrow slit and tried to look around.

He lay on his back on something hard. When he saw iron bars off to one side, he figured out that he was in a jail cell, probably lying on the bunk. He had been carried in here and dumped on the bunk, still unconscious from being walloped with the butt of that greener wielded by Sheriff Thacker. Somebody had tossed his hat onto his chest. It fell off and landed on the floor as he rolled over and swung his legs off the bunk. His shrieking muscles didn't want to cooperate, but he forced them to.

He sat hunched over for a long moment, his head cradled gingerly in his hands. He was so dizzy that the world seemed to be spinning the wrong way. As he waited for it to settle down and start turning properly, he tried to figure out what had happened.

The cobwebs gradually cleared from his brain. Sheriff Thacker must have gotten reports of a brawl going on in the Cattle King. When he had rushed in and seen Longarm standing in the middle of the destruction, he had reacted as a lawman and moved to subdue the man he blamed for the fracas. He hadn't taken any chances, either, striking hard and fast with the butt of the shotgun before anybody had a chance to explain that Longarm had only been defending himself from Brice MacPhail.

Even though he'd been out cold, Longarm had no trouble imagining the scene after that. Thacker had taken Longarm into custody, ignoring the protests that Walt Conroy and Charlie probably made. Longarm wondered if the sheriff had arrested MacPhail, too.

A deep groan from somewhere nearby prompted Longarm to turn his head, and he saw the answer to his question. MacPhail lay on the bunk in the next cell. He was still unconscious, but he was beginning to stir a little.

Well, at least Thacker hadn't singled him out, Longarm told himself. That was scant comfort, though. Things were coming to a head in Medallion. The case that had brought him here would likely bust wide open in a matter of hours—maybe even sooner, because he didn't know how long he'd been unconscious—and yet here he was, stuck in a jail cell, helpless to do anything to stop the hell that was planned.

Even though his head hurt like blazes, he was thinking straight, and he had pretty much the whole picture now. There were still a few holes, and some of what he had come up with was pure speculation, but his instincts told him he was right. The biggest question that remained was what the hell he could do about it.

He reached up with a shaky hand and pried his left eye open, pulling out a couple of eyelashes in the process. The pain caused tears to form in his eyes, and that washed away some of the dried blood. He blinked rapidly until his vision cleared up. Then he got to his feet and went over to clutch the bars of the cell door.

There was a narrow hallway on the other side of the bars, leading to a heavy wooden door with a single barred window in it. That would be the door between the cell block and the sheriff's office, Longarm knew. He shook the cell door, rattling it loudly, and shouted, "Sheriff! Sheriff Thacker!"

A few moments went by, and Longarm was beginning to think that Thacker wasn't in the office. But then a key rattled in the lock of the cell block door, and it swung back. Thacker's bulky silhouette appeared in the opening.

"Shut up in there!" the sheriff snapped. "You go to raising a ruckus and I won't let you out come morning."

"Sheriff, you've got to listen to me." Longarm glanced at the barred window in the cell and saw that it was gray with dusk. Night was coming on in a hurry, and that knowledge added to the feeling of urgency that gnawed at Longarm. "You've got to let me out of here. There are things going on that you don't know about."

Thacker snorted. "I know that you and MacPhail caused a heap of damage in the Cattle King. You'll dig deep in your pockets to pay it off in the morning. Otherwise the judge will probably keep you behind bars for a month or two."

"Damn it, Sheriff—" Longarm stopped short and took a deep breath, reining in his temper.

If he got angry it would probably just make Thacker more stubborn than ever. The only good thing about the situation was that the sheriff was acting like a heavy-handed but basically honest lawman. Maybe he could be reasoned with.

"Listen, Sheriff," Longarm began again, "I'm a lawman, too."

157

"Yeah, Walt Conroy said he'd hired you as a range detective while he and his sister were trying to talk me out of arresting you. But a range detective ain't a real lawman in my book, Parker, so you can forget about that."

"I'm not a range detective," Longarm said stubbornly. "I'm a deputy United States marshal. And my name ain't Parker, it's Long. Custis Long." He hurried on, trying to get all the words out before Thacker could interrupt. "I work for Chief Marshal Billy Vail out of the Denver office. You can wire him and check on my story if you want."

Curious in spite of himself, Thacker came closer. "A U.S. marshal?" he repeated. "Where's your badge?"

"I don't have it," Longarm admitted grimly. "Somebody stole it, along with my other bona fides. But that's who I really am." A thought occurred to him. "There's somebody right here in Medallion who can confirm that I'm a federal lawman, too. Find old Salty, the stagecoach driver, and ask him. He knows the truth."

"I'm supposed to believe an addlepated old pelican like him?" Thacker shook his head. "If you want to stick to that story, Parker, I'll wire Denver in the morning. Until then, just settle down and don't make things worse for yourself."

"Damn it!" Longarm burst out, unable to contain himself. "I can't wait until tomorrow. All hell's gonna break loose tonight!"

Thacker stepped closer to the bars, a scowl on his face. "What the devil are you talking about?"

Instead of answering the question, Longarm asked one of his own. "Where's your deputy?"

That took Thacker by surprise. He frowned in confusion and said, "You mean Dave Bardwell? I reckon he's around town somewhere. He doesn't come on duty until ten o'clock."

"By then it'll be all over, and Bardwell and the rest of his gang will be long gone."

"Gang! Now I know you're crazy! You're talking about Dave like he's some sort of owlhoot."

"That's exactly what he is," Longarm insisted. "He's the ringleader of the gang that's been hitting those gold shipments and rustling cattle from the Triangle C."

Thacker stared at Longarm as if the big lawman had just grown a second head. "What in blazes are you talking about?"

The story was too long and complicated to explain easily, but Longarm wasn't going to get the chance to try it. Before he could say anything, heavy footsteps sounded in the sheriff's office.

Thacker turned toward the cell block door and put his hand on the butt of the pistol holstered at his waist. "Who's out there?" he called warily.

"It's Walt Conroy, Sheriff," came the reply. "I want to talk to you about Parker."

Thacker blew out his breath in frustration. With a glare at Longarm, he turned away and walked up the corridor to the office.

Thacker left the door open, so Longarm was able to hear as the sheriff said, "I already told you, Walt, Parker and MacPhail got to stay in jail until the judge can hold a hearing tomorrow morning. He'll set the damages, and if they can pay, I'll let 'em loose."

"I don't give a damn about MacPhail," Conroy said. "He doesn't work for me anymore, and you can keep him locked up until Kingdom Come for all I care. But I've talked to Jasper Riggins, the owner of the Cattle King, and settled all the damages with him."

"You paid the damages?" Thacker asked.

"That's right. So you have no more reason to hold Parker."

"What about disturbing the peace? There's likely to be some charges for that, and a fine, too."

"I'll pay it," Conroy said. "Just tell me how much, and I'll pay it."

"The judge will have to decide that," Thacker said stubbornly.

Conroy's carefully controlled temper slipped a little. "Damn it, Sheriff . . . you're determined to keep Parker locked up, aren't you, even though the fight wasn't his fault?"

"I know you said MacPhail started it. That don't mean Parker had to fight back."

"What would you have had him do? What kind of man are you, to think he could walk away from that?"

Longarm grimaced. Insulting Thacker's manhood probably wasn't a good idea.

Sure enough, the sheriff said, "That's about enough, Conroy! I know you've got the biggest spread in these parts, but I won't be talked to like that. Parker stays behind bars, and that's that!"

"You'd let him out if Jessup asked you to."

"You'd better go," Thacker said coldly.

Longarm heard the sound of footsteps, and then the cell block door slammed shut again. The key turned in the lock with a sound of finality. As far as Thacker was concerned, Longarm wasn't getting out until morning.

And that would be too late.

He paced back and forth for several minutes after Conroy left, knowing that it wouldn't do any good but unable to keep from doing so. He thought that if he had to sit in this cell all night, he might go plumb loco. He was about to yell at Thacker again, even though he knew it would be futile, when he heard a voice at the cell window.

"Psst! Custis!"

Longarm turned sharply to the window. It was a little higher than eye level, so he turned over the unused slops bucket and stood on it to look out, grasping the bars as he did so.

Charlie Conroy peered in at him. She was on horseback, so she could see through the window. Night had fallen while first Longarm and then Walt Conroy talked with Sheriff Thacker, but even in the gloom of the alley behind the jail, Charlie's blond hair shone.

"Charlie!" Longarm said. "What are you doing here?"

"We're going to get you out of there, Custis," she said. "You didn't do anything wrong, and it ain't right you're locked up."

"Your brother was here a few minutes ago, trying to talk some sense into the sheriff—"

"I know. Walt told me he didn't do any good. Thacker's gonna keep you locked up, even though Walt already paid off the damages." Charlie laughed. "Or at least he thinks he's gonna keep you locked up."

"Charlie, there's nothing you can do about this."

"The hell there ain't." There was a faint clanking sound as she held up a chain. "Loop this around the bars. We've got a singletree out here it's attached to, and six horses to pull it. Those bars are coming out, and some of the wall with them, I'll bet."

She was probably right about that, but Longarm hesitated anyway. "Who's with you out there?"

"Just some of the boys from the Triangle C."

"What about your brother?"

Charlie laughed again. "Walt doesn't know anything about this. He's mad at Thacker, but he'd draw the line at a jailbreak. So a couple of the hands are keeping him busy over at the saloon."

"Charlie, I don't think this is a good idea—"

"The hell it ain't. Listen, Custis, Brice MacPhail's nothing but a damn bully. He's been throwing his weight around at the Triangle C for a long time. But you handing him his needin's tonight made you a friend of every man in the crew. We want to do this for you."

Longarm looked past her, saw the dark figures of the

horses and their riders waiting to bust him out of jail. They were just asking for trouble by helping him . . . and yet, he couldn't pass up the chance to get out of here. He had things to do tonight. As for any charges that might be brought against Charlie and the Triangle C punchers . . . well, once he was able to establish his identity as a federal lawman, he could intercede with the local authorities and maybe get any charges against them dropped.

"All right," he said. "Lemme see that chain."

He looped it around the four iron bars that blocked the window and handed it back to Charlie. She took the end of it back to the singletree that lay on the ground and fastened it securely. The cowboys had tied their lariats to the singletree, and when they urged their horses forward, the ropes and the chain all grew taut, lifting the singletree from the ground. Charlie backed her horse off to the side, well out of the way.

The chain grew tighter and tighter around the bars. Longarm could see that in the light from the one oil lamp that hung in the cell block. He heard a grinding sound and knew that the mortar around the bars was starting to give way. The jail had stone walls, and cracks began to appear around some of the rocks.

From the next cell, Brice MacPhail suddenly called, "Hey! Hey, what the hell's goin' on over there?"

"Shut up," Longarm growled at him. Longarm picked up his hat and put it on as the bars bent and shifted some more.

"Son of a bitch! Somebody's breakin' you out!" MacPhail was sitting up on his bunk now, staring as he looked over into Longarm's cell. Suddenly, his features twisted in hatred, and he bellowed, "Sheriff! Help! Jailbreak!"

Longarm lunged at the bars between the cells and reached through them, trying to get a hand on MacPhail, but he couldn't reach that far. MacPhail grinned evilly and yelled again, "Jailbreak!"

Outside, the cowboys urged their horses on, and with a crash the rocks and mortar suddenly gave way and the bars flew out of the window, taking large chunks of masonry with them. The gap that was left was barely wide enough for Longarm's broad shoulders, but he didn't have time to try to widen it. He thrust his arms through the aperture and began to climb out.

"Hey!" Sheriff Thacker yelled from somewhere behind him. "Hey! Stop! Stop or I'll shoot!"

The sides of the opening scraped painfully on Longarm's hide as he pulled himself through. He got stuck momentarily and had a horrible vision of the sheriff blasting his backside full of buckshot, and that probably made him struggle a little harder to writhe through the busted-out window. Strong hands grabbed him and pulled, and he popped through it like a watermelon seed.

At that instant, a shotgun roared inside the jail. Some of the buckshot peppered the wall of the cell around the window, while the rest of the charge tore through the opening where Longarm had been a hair's-breadth of time earlier. All the pellets missed him, though, as he fell to the alley under the window.

Charlie spurred up beside him, leading a riderless horse. "Get on!" she called.

Longarm scrambled to his feet, grabbed the horn and swung up into the saddle. The Triangle C hands had already cut loose from the singletree and were galloping away into the night. As soon as Longarm hit leather, he snatched off his hat and swatted Charlie's horse on the rump.

"Get outta here!" he snapped. Charlie's horse lunged away.

Longarm rode after her. Behind him, Sheriff Thacker had gotten the cell door unlocked and run inside the cell to thrust the barrel of the greener out the window. He triggered the second barrel, but by the time the scattergun boomed, Longarm was too far away, riding hard and bent low in the saddle.

Well, he was a fugitive again, he told himself, just like early that morning when he had awakened with Regina Jessup's dead body next to him in bed. He wasn't sure where the murdered redhead had gotten off to, but he had a pretty good idea. He was headed there himself.

As he and Charlie reached Medallion's main street, Longarm swung his mount toward the brightly lighted mansion overlooking the settlement.

He had a party to attend.

Chapter 19

As he rode toward the Jessup house, the sound of hoof-beats made him look over. Charlie had pulled alongside him and was riding hard to keep up. She passed him a six-gun that he took and pouched in his empty holster.

"Damn it, go back to town!" Longarm called to her when he was armed again.

"No, I'm staying with you, Custis!" she said over the pounding of hoofbeats. "Where are we going?"

There was no time to explain, and he knew that he couldn't force Charlie to leave him alone. But he was riding into danger and didn't want to have to be looking after her, either.

Before he could argue, a group of men appeared in the roadway ahead of them, walking toward Medallion. Longarm and Charlie were forced to rein in sharply to avoid trampling the men.

"Dadgummit, watch where you're goin'!" the leader of the bunch shouted as dust billowed up from the sliding hooves of the two horses. "Like to run over us, you danged whippersnappers!"

"Salty!" Longarm exclaimed.

"Custis?" Salty hurried forward. "Is that you?"

"What are you doing here?" Longarm asked. "Are these the guards you hired? You're supposed to be up at the Jessup place!"

"Mr. Jessup his ownself fired us!" Salty explained. "Told us we wasn't needed after all and said we should come back to town. I asked him where you were, but he wouldn't tell me. I didn't much want to leave, but didn't figure there was really anything else we could do."

The fact that Jessup had sent Salty and the other men away tied in with the suspicions that had formed in Longarm's mind. He said, "Is the party getting started up there?"

"Damn straight it is." Salty glanced at Charlie and added, "Pardon my language, Miss Conroy."

"I don't give a damn about your language," Charlie said. "Custis, what's going on here?"

Longarm ignored her question and asked Salty, "Jessup's guests have started to arrive?"

"Yep. All the mine owners from these parts are there, along with their families. And some bankers and politicians and such-like from Kingman and Flagstaff, too. They come up in private coaches and buggies."

Longarm bit back a curse. Everything was in place, and it was just a matter of time before hell began to pop.

As a matter of fact, the faint sound of a gunshot came to his ears at that moment. Longarm lifted his head and stared toward the mansion, but the shot wasn't repeated.

"What in blazes?" Salty said.

There was no time to explain. Longarm said, "Salty, if you and these boys don't mind wading into a mess of trouble, follow me up to the Jessup house. Get there as quick as you can, but don't go in until I give you the word!"

"All right, Custis," Salty said, but Longarm was already galloping toward the mansion, with Charlie right behind him.

He knew the outlaws would have left some guards out,

so he reined to a halt and swung down from the saddle while he was still a couple of hundred yards short of the Jessup house. Charlie followed his example.

"Can you use that six-shooter on your hip?" he asked her in a whisper.

"Damn right I can."

Longarm wasn't surprised, considering the way she had lit into those rustlers. "Stay behind me and follow my lead," he told her.

Charlie nodded. Longarm wasn't sure she would be so cooperative when they got up to the mansion, but he had to take that chance. Time was running out.

He left the road and made his way up the hill through some trees and brush, moving as quietly as possible. Charlie tagged along behind him. When they drew near the mansion, Longarm dropped to a crouch and eased forward. Sure enough, there were two men with rifles posted at the front door. They wore dusters and had hoods under their Stetsons, covering their faces except for the eyeholes.

Quite a few carriages and buggies were parked in the drive in front of the house. Longarm saw a few sprawled shapes lying on the ground near them and knew those were the drivers of those vehicles. Whether they were dead or just knocked out, he didn't know, and there was no time to check.

"If we could jump those guards some way and take those dusters and hoods . . ." Longarm began.

Charlie pointed to the shrubbery that flanked the front door. "Slip up through those bushes," she whispered. "I'll distract them, and you can jump them and knock them out."

"How in hell—"

Charlie's fingers went to the buttons of her shirt. "Leave that to me," she breathed.

Longarm frowned. It seemed to him that she was taking an awful chance, and yet he could see how her hastily conceived plan might work. He gave her a curt nod and moved off to the right, looping around through the shrubs and flower beds, thankful for the elaborate landscaping that provided so much cover.

Moving as silently as an Indian, he approached to within ten feet of the sentries without them having any idea he was there. He had been in position for less than a minute when Charlie strode into view, timing her entrance perfectly. As she walked into the circle of light cast by the lamps over the front door, one of the guards exclaimed, "Hey! Who the hell—"

Then he fell silent, because, like his partner, he was too busy staring at Charlie Conroy's bare breasts. She had removed her shirt and gunbelt before walking up to the mansion, and the firm, proud, brown-nippled globes that rode high on her chest drew the rapt gazes of the two men like a lodestone attracted iron filings.

The distraction worked for only a second, but that was long enough. The sentries didn't see Longarm lunging at them until it was too late. The one nearest him tried to turn, but the butt of Longarm's Colt crashed down on his head even as his mouth was opening to loose a yell. The man's knees unhinged and he fell limply to the flagstone porch, out cold.

Charlie took care of the other guard, snatching her revolver from behind her back and pistol-whipping the man across his masked face. There was a crunch of bone shattering as the blow landed solidly. He dropped his rifle and reached for his broken jaw. Longarm's gun butt crashed against his skull and sent him toppling into unconsciousness.

The big lawman holstered his Colt and started yanking dusters and hoods off the two men as fast as he could. He tossed one of the long coats to Charlie. She put it on and buttoned it up, concealing the fact that under it she was nude from the waist up. Longarm shrugged into the other duster. They pulled the hoods over their heads and put on the guards' hats. Then they picked up the fallen rifles and went into the house, with Longarm leading the way.

He had fought side by side with several women in the past, most notably the beautiful and deadly Jessie Starbuck from over Texas way. Charlie Conroy showed signs of being the equal of any of them. He was still worried about her safety, but at the same time he was glad to have her for an ally.

Longarm's face turned grim under the hood as he saw the bloody, crumpled body of the servant named Lee lying on the parquet floor of the foyer. Lee was still breathing, but he appeared to have been shot a couple of times. Longarm hoped medical attention would get to him in time to save his life.

At the moment, there were other lives to save. Silently, Longarm and Charlie approached the entrance to the big ballroom. The doors stood slightly open, so they could hear and even see a little of what was going on inside.

Several masked, duster-clad owlhoots stood on one side of the room with rifles in their hands, menacing the crowd of fancy-dressed guests who had been herded to the other side of the room.

One of the outlaws stood in front of the others. He was saying to the prisoners: "—all your money and valuables, especially the ladies' jewelry. And we'll be takin' some of you with us, so there won't be anybody chasin' after us. Don't worry, though. If your families pay the ransom, nobody will get hurt."

Victor Jessup stood off to one side, his face pale and haggard. He had been forced to go along with this audacious scheme, and Longarm had a pretty good idea what sort of leverage had been used against him.

"Now toss the loot in the bags my boys are carryin'," the boss outlaw said as a couple of members of the gang moved forward with canvas bags in their hands. "Don't try anything, because if you do, we *will* kill you."

Longarm knew the voice. It belonged to Dave Bardwell, of course. Bardwell had been ramrodding the gang from the start, using the inside knowledge he had gained from his position as deputy to learn when gold shipments would be leaving the Oro Grande. He had been behind the rustling, too, knowing that Walt Conroy was eager to blame all the trouble on Jessup's miners. The gang had even held up the stagecoach bringing Jessup and his wife to Medallion, probably in hopes of kidnapping Regina and forcing Jessup to pay a huge ransom for her return.

They probably would have been disappointed if they had been successful in snatching her, Longarm thought.

But after he had ruined that for the gang and the stage had traveled on to Medallion, Regina had announced the plans for this party, and an even bolder scheme had been born. Why hold up one rich man and his wife when you could hold up a whole damn roomful of them? This would be the big cleanup, the crowning job after which the gang would flee this part of the country. And as things had worked out, they had even been able to force Victor Jessup to cooperate with them.

Longarm put his mouth close to Charlie's ear and whispered through the hoods, "Salty and his bunch will be here any minute. Go back outside and meet them. Send them around to the other side of the house, where all those French doors are. When the shooting starts, they can bust in that way."

"What are you going to do?" she asked.

"Try to draw that bunch off a little so that those folks in there won't be as likely to get hit by stray bullets when all hell breaks loose."

Charlie nodded. She slipped back along the hallway toward the front door and went out into the night

Longarm waited a few minutes, during which time the outlaws continued to collect money and valuables from the prisoners. He kept a close eye on the French doors. Finally

170

he saw movement in the shadows, and a second later Charlie and Salty moved into the edge of the light for a second, just long enough to let him know that they were out there. Charlie still wore the duster but had taken off the hood and hat so that Salty and his companions would know she wasn't one of the outlaws.

Longarm took a deep breath and threw the doors of the ballroom wide open. This trick had worked once, he thought. No reason it couldn't work again. He stepped into the room and yelled, "Shit, there's a posse right outside the front door!"

He could see now that there were fully a dozen masked outlaws in the room. They swung around in alarm, and Bardwell rapped at them, "Get out there and stop them!" The men surged toward the double doors. Longarm stepped aside to let them pass.

The outlaws were at the ballroom entrance when Bardwell suddenly yelled, "Wait a minute! That's not Cal or Frank!"

Longarm didn't know what had given him away, but it didn't matter. The owlhoots were bunched together, well away from the frightened party guests. He leaped to the side, knocking his hat off and ripping the hood from his head with one hand as he brought the rifle up with the other. "Now, Salty!" he bellowed, then lined the Winchester on Bardwell and fired one-handed.

As the rifle cracked, the guests screamed, yelled and either hit the floor or ducked for cover. Glass crashed as Charlie, Salty and the men they had brought with them burst in through the French doors, guns blazing.

The slug from Longarm's rifle struck Bardwell and staggered him, but he stayed on his feet and triggered twice at the big lawman. A fancy vase on a side table exploded into a million pieces as one of the bullets struck it, and Longarm felt as much as heard the wind-rip of the other slug as it passed close by his ear. He slapped his left hand on the Winchester's breech as he worked the lever. He fired three times from the hip, as fast as he could jack fresh rounds into the chamber.

The bullets tore into Bardwell, driving him back in a grotesque dance. Still, he managed to hang on to his revolver and even lifted it to get off a dying shot.

The slug from Bardwell's gun didn't travel very far. It slammed into the midsection of Victor Jessup, who was charging at Bardwell and screaming curses at the top of his lungs. Even hit as he was, Jessup's momentum carried him forward, and he crashed into Bardwell. Both men went down. Jessup's hands locked around Bardwell's neck. The mine owner shuddered as he died, but he kept his stranglehold on Bardwell's throat, even though it was no longer necessary.

Taken by surprise, the other outlaws tried to swing around and confront the unexpected threat from their rear, but Charlie, Salty and the rest of the group that came in through the French doors poured bullets at them in a veritable storm of lead. Half a dozen of the masked owlhoots went down in the first volley, and although they got a few shots off, they weren't able to put up much resistance before three more men were knocked off their feet to lie in huddled shapes on the floor, bloodstains spreading on their dusters and on the hoods that concealed their death-contorted features.

The other three outlaws saw that the situation was hopeless. They threw their guns down and thrust their arms in the air. One of them yelled, "Don't shoot! We give up!"

Gradually, the echoes of the brief but fierce battle faded away. Silence descended on the room, broken only by the terrified whimpering of some of the party guests, who were still hugging the floor or crouching behind pieces of furniture.

Longarm worked the Winchester's lever. The ejected cartridge rattled and spun on the brightly polished wooden floor. He called to the frightened guests, "It's all over, folks. You can get up now."

One man, beefy and white-haired with the look of a politician about him, demanded shakily, "Who are you, sir?"

"Deputy United States Marshal Custis Long," Longarm introduced himself. He saw the startled look on Charlie's face. Salty just chuckled. There was no more need for subterfuge.

Limping a little, Charlie walked over to Longarm, reloading her Colt as she crossed the room. "You're a lawman for real?" she asked.

"That's right." Longarm nodded toward her injured leg. "Did you break that wound open again?"

"Damn it, no. I wish everybody would quit worrying about that. The leg's just a little sore, that's all." She holstered her gun and stepped closer to Longarm. "A little exercise isn't going to hurt it, if you know what I mean." She toyed teasingly with the top button of the duster that hid her partial nudity.

Longarm sighed, grinned, and shook his head. "After we get all this mess cleaned up, I might just take you up on that."

Chapter 20

"I still think I ought to throw you back in a cell," Sheriff Rip Thacker said in a surly voice as he glared at Longarm. "I'm willing to listen, though. You just better have a good explanation for everything, Parker. I mean, Long."

Several hours had passed, and during that time a flurry of emergency telegrams had gone back and forth between Medallion and Denver. Even though Longarm's badge and bona fides hadn't turned up, Thacker was willing—although still a little reluctant—to accept the fact that Longarm was a federal lawman. Billy Vail's telegrams had convinced him of that, along with Salty's testimony to that fact.

Now Longarm sat in the sheriff's office with Thacker, Salty and Walt, as well as Charlie Conroy. They all watched him as he began to lay out the story he had pieced together from his own theories and the information he had gotten from questioning the captured outlaws.

"Dave Bardwell was the ramrod of the gang from the start, but the raid on Jessup's party tonight was the first time he'd actually taken part in any of the jobs. The rest of the time he just passed on information about the ore shipments and told the gang when and where to wide-loop Triangle C cattle. He's the one who found that trail through the badlands, too, when he was chasing an outlaw one time, back before he turned crooked. But it was finding that trail and realizing it would be a good way to get stolen cows out of the area that gave him the idea to become an outlaw.

"Bardwell wasn't the only boss in the gang, though. He had a partner who actually did a lot of the planning: Connie Maxwell."

Conroy shook his head. "That's hard to believe. She was a fine singer, and she seemed so . . . I don't know . . . innocent."

"She never struck me that way," Charlie said with a snort of disgust. "A woman can always tell when another woman is on the shady side. I've been suspicious of her for a long time."

Longarm sort of doubted that, but he didn't argue the point. He went on, "Connie was probably just as important a source of information about the ore shipments as Bardwell was, since she was having an affair with Jessup. In fact, he snuck into her room at the Cattle King early this morning, while I was lying low there after Connie and Bardwell tried to frame me for Mrs. Jessup's murder. I heard his voice, but I didn't recognize it and put two and two together until later."

Sheriff Thacker leaned forward and clasped his hands together on his desk. "You mean Jessup came sniffing around that saloon singer not long after he murdered his own wife? That snake-blooded so-and-so."

Longarm shook his head and said, "I don't reckon Jessup murdered Regina."

"But we found her body up at the mansion, hidden in a closet," Thacker said with a frown.

"Yeah, but I believe it was Bardwell who took her up there after the frame-up didn't work. He blackmailed Jessup into cooperating with the gang about the holdup at the party, by threatening to arrest Jessup for Regina's murder. He could claim he found the body there and lay the blame for the whole thing on Jessup." Longarm's face was grim as he added, "Connie and Bardwell got a lot of use out of that corpse. They used it to try to frame me, and then they used it to pressure Jessup into going along with them. When the guests started arriving for the party, he probably strung them along with some story about how his wife wasn't feeling well and would be down later, until everybody was there and the gang was ready to strike."

"All that's probably true," Thacker said, "but it still doesn't tell us who killed Regina Jessup."

Longarm got a reflective look on his face as he said, "We may never know for sure unless we catch up with her, but I'm thinking Connie Maxwell did that. I wonder if Regina found out about Connie's affair with her husband and came to see her to tell her to leave Jessup alone. They could have fought, and if Connie had grabbed a knife and cut Regina's throat, she and Bardwell would have had to do something with her body. That must have happened not long after she slipped me the knockout drops."

"Why did she do that?" Charlie asked. "And what were you doing with . . . Oh, never mind. I reckon I know the answer to that."

Longarm answered the first question and ignored the one Charlie had started to ask. "Bardwell didn't like the looks of me right from the start. Maybe he was just the naturally suspicious type, or maybe we crossed trails sometime in the past and he thought he remembered me. Either way, I reckon it was him who told Connie to give me those knockout drops and then search me. She found my badge and bona fides, and then she and Bardwell knew they'd have to do something to get rid of me, because they didn't want a federal lawman nosing around."

He didn't add that the conspirators hadn't been worried about Thacker discovering what was going on. The sheriff could draw that conclusion for himself, if he wanted to, without Longarm pointing it out.

Walt Conroy said, "In that case, why didn't they just kill you and dump your body in an alley or something?"

"I reckon they might have," Longarm said, "but I think that's when Regina Jessup showed up. After she wound up dead, Connie and Bardwell had two bodies on their hands: Regina's and mine, only I was just unconscious, not dead. That was when they decided to get fancy and use Regina to frame me. If I was found in bed with her corpse, nobody would believe that I hadn't killed her or that I was a deputy marshal, because they had taken my credentials. Once I was behind bars, some of Bardwell's gang would have come into town and stirred up a lynch mob to take me out of the jail and string me up."

"They might have tried to," Thacker growled. "They wouldn't have gotten away with it."

Longarm had his doubts about that, but again, he didn't say anything on that matter. He continued, "Of course, they tried to cover all the possible angles by posting a gunman in the alley behind the hotel, in case I managed to get out of there before I could be arrested. That didn't work, either. With me on the loose, Regina's body wasn't any use to Bardwell and Connie as long as it was in the hotel, so Bardwell got rid of all the evidence and took the corpse up to the mansion, where he used it to blackmail Jessup."

"And Jessup just let him get away with that?" Charlie asked. "For God's sake, his wife was dead!"

"Yeah, but he didn't really care about that," Longarm said. "He was probably glad to get rid of her, since she'd been blackmailing him for years, too, ever since she forced him to marry her in the first place."

Walt Conroy threw his hands in the air. "Good God,

Marshal! How much more of this infernally convoluted tale is there?"

Longarm grinned as he said, "Not much. I knew that Jessup had been putting up with Regina's, uh, wayward ways, so to speak, for a long time, and I asked myself why. Seemed to be a reasonable assumption that she had something she was holding over his head. So when my boss and I started wiring messages back and forth this evening, I asked him to do some checking on Jessup. I reckon Billy must've woke up some important folks back East somewhere. He can really scorch those telegraph wires when he wants to. The whole story ain't come out yet, but it looks like Jessup wasn't the fella's real name. Turns out he killed a fella and stole a bunch of money back in Pennsylvania, and that's what bankrolled his mining business when he came West and changed his name. Billy ought to have all the details about that in a day or two, but we know enough now we can figure that Regina knew about it, too, and that's how she got Jessup to go along with whatever she wanted to do."

Thacker asked hoarsely, "Is that all?"

Longarm leaned back in his chair, cocked his right ankle on his left knee and took out a cheroot. Before putting it in his mouth, he said, "Yeah, it took a heap of bites, but I reckon all the apple is just about et." He paused and added, "Except for Connie."

"Nobody's seen her," Thacker said. "She didn't put on her show at the Cattle King tonight."

Longarm snapped a lucifer to life and lit the cheroot. Around the gasper clenched in his choppers, he said, "That don't surprise me none. She was probably supposed to meet up with Bardwell somewhere after the holdup at the mansion, and they'd take off for the tall and uncut with their share of the loot. When Bardwell didn't show up, she knew something had gone wrong." He shook his head. "Chances are, we'll never see her again."

"Good riddance," Charlie said.

Longarm couldn't argue with that, although it pained him to think that Connie might escape the justice that was coming to her. But there was no denying it: Connie Maxwell was living proof that sometimes evil came in cute little packages as well as big ugly ones.

Under the circumstances, the management at the Horton House was happy to give Longarm a different room. He was there now, well after midnight, lying in bed with a nude and very satisfied Charlotte Conroy. Nude, that is, except for the bandages wrapped around her wounded leg. They had made love carefully, with Charlie on top, riding him slowly and sensuously until the end, when they had both gotten a mite carried away. Charlie's leg was fine, though. So was the rest of her, in Longarm's humble opinion.

He filled his hand with one of her breasts as she lay there with her head pillowed on his shoulder. Her lips nuzzled his skin warmly. She whispered, "When will you have to leave, Custis?"

"I imagine I'll take the stage to Kingman tomorrow and start back to Denver from there," Longarm answered honestly. "That is, if ol' Salty will have me for a passenger. For some reason, he seems to think that trouble follows me around." He paused for a second and then added, "I'm sorry I can't stay longer. I reckon Billy Vail will have a new job for me as soon as I get back, though."

Charlie propped herself up on an elbow. "You don't reckon I'm all upset about you leavin', do you, Custis? I mean, I'm a mite fond of you and all, but I sure as hell ain't ready to tie myself down to one man!"

"Well," Longarm said with a rueful chuckle, "that's mighty good to know."

She snuggled against his shoulder again. He didn't say anything about it, and neither did she, but he was pretty sure he had seen the faint sparkle of tears in her eyes, despite what she'd said.

They lay there like that for quite a while, and Longarm was about to doze off when he heard a couple of faint noises. One of them was the squeak of a floorboard, the other a barely audible rasp of metal on metal as a key was slid stealthily into the lock on the door . . .

His muscles jolted into action as he rolled toward the side of the bed away from the door, taking Charlie with him. She cried out, startled out of the light sleep into which she had fallen while in Longarm's embrace. His free hand slapped the butt of the Colt on the chair next to the bed. He dragged the gun out of its holster as they fell to the floor.

The door flew open and huge gouts of Colt flame bloomed in the darkness. The bullets tore through the bed where Longarm and Charlie had been lying. The small, slender figure in the doorway had to use both hands to hold the revolver as it bucked and blasted. Over the roar of the shots, Connie Maxwell shrieked, "You ruined everything! Everything!"

She was no songbird now. Her voice was shrill, ugly.

Eyes narrowed against the glare of the muzzle flashes, Longarm took aim and fired. Connie cried out as the bullet raked along the outside of her forearm. The gun in her hands went spinning away from her.

Charlie lunged up off the floor and across the room. She was considerably taller and heavier than Connie, and she was as fierce as a Valkyrie as she uncorked a punch that landed cleanly on Connie's jaw. The impact threw Connie back across the hall, where she bounced off the door of the room opposite and pitched face forward to the floor of the corridor. Charlie glared down at Connie's insensible form and said, "I never did cotton much to her."

Longarm holstered his Colt and reached for his pants.

He had to stop himself from laughing as he said to Charlie, "Better get some clothes on. All them shots'll draw a heap of attention, and now that Connie's gonna do all her singing behind bars, folks may be hankering for some other sort of show."

Watch for

**LONGARM AND THE
APACHE WAR**

the 330th novel in the exciting LONGARM
series from Jove

Coming in May!

LONGARM

Explore the exciting Old West with one of the men who made it wild!

GIANT-SIZED ADVENTURE FROM AVENGING ANGEL LONGARM.

LONGARM AND THE DEADLY DEAD MAN
0-515-13547-X
THIS ALL-NEW, GIANT-SIZED ADVENTURE IN THE POPULAR ALL-ACTION SERIES PUTS THE "WILD" BACK IN THE WILD WEST—AND PROVES THAT A DEAD OUTLAW IS SAFER IN HIS GRAVE THAN FACING AN AVENGING ANGEL NAMED LONGARM.

LONGARM AND THE BARTERED BRIDES
0-515-13834-7
SOME MEN, ACHING FOR FEMALE COMPANIONSHIP, HAVE SENT AWAY FOR BRIDES. BUT WHEN THE WOMENFOLK NEVER SHOW, THESE HOMBRES HIRE ON GUNSLINGER CUSTIS LONG TO DO WHAT HE DOES SECOND-BEST: SKIRT-CHASING.

AVAILABLE WHEREVER BOOKS ARE SOLD OR AT PENGUIN.COM

GIANT ACTION! GIANT ADVENTURE!

THE GUNSMITH

GIANT

Giant Westerns featuring The Gunsmith

The Ghost of Billy the Kid
0-515-13622-0

**Little Sureshot and the
Wild West Show**
0-515-13851-7

Dead Weight
0-515-14028-7

Available wherever books are sold or at
penguin.com

J799

J. R. ROBERTS

THE GUNSMITH

THE GUNSMITH #268: BIG-SKY BANDITS	0-515-13717-0
THE GUNSMITH #269: THE HANGING TREE	0-515-13735-9
THE GUNSMITH #270: THE BIG FORK GAME	0-515-13752-9
THE GUNSMITH #271: IN FOR A POUND	0-515-13775-8
THE GUNSMITH #272: DEAD-END PASS	0-515-13796-0
THE GUNSMITH #273: TRICKS OF THE TRADE	0-515-13814-2
THE GUNSMITH #274: GUILTY AS CHARGED	0-515-13837-1
THE GUNSMITH #275: THE LUCKY LADY	0-515-13854-1
THE GUNSMITH #276: THE CANADIAN JOB	0-515-13860-6
THE GUNSMITH #277: ROLLING THUNDER	0-515-13878-9
THE GUNSMITH #278: THE HANGING JUDGE	0-515-13889-4
THE GUNSMITH #279: DEATH IN DENVER	0-515-13901-7
THE GUNSMITH #280: THE RECKONING	0-515-13935-1
THE GUNSMITH #281: RING OF FIRE	0-515-13945-9
THE GUNSMITH #282: THE LAST RIDE	0-515-13957-2
THE GUNSMITH #283: RIDING THE WHIRLWIND	0-515-13967-X
THE GUNSMITH #284: SCORPION'S TALE	0-515-13988-2
THE GUNSMITH #285: INNOCENT BLOOD	0-515-14012-0
THE GUNSMITH #286: THE GHOST OF GOLIAD	0-515-14020-1
THE GUNSMITH #287: THE REAPERS	0-515-14031-7
THE GUNSMITH #288: THE DEADLY AND THE DIVINE	0-515-14044-9
THE GUNSMITH #289: AMAZON GOLD	0-515-14056-2
THE GUNSMITH #290: THE GRAND PRIZE	0-515-14070-8
THE GUNSMITH #291: GUNMAN'S CROSSING	0-515-14092-9